THE DAYS
OF THE
BITTER END

A Novel by

JACK ENGELHARD

The 1960s recaptured… A colossal masterpiece of historical fiction from Jack Engelhard. This is his War and Peace.

DayRay Literary Press
British Columbia, Canada

The Days of the Bitter End

Copyright ©1998, 2001, 2013, 2025 by Jack Engelhard
ISBN-13 978-1-77143-103-3
Third Edition, Revised

Library and Archives Canada Cataloguing in Publication
Engelhard, Jack, 1940-, author
The days of the Bitter End / by Jack Engelhard. – Third edition.
Issued in print and electronic formats.
ISBN 978-1-77143-103-3 (pbk.).--ISBN 978-1-77143-104-0 (pdf)
Additional cataloguing data available from Library and Archives Canada

Jack Engelhard may be contacted through: **www.jackengelhard.com**

Cover artwork: Photo of Jack Engelhard © Jack Engelhard.

Previously published in 2001 by Comteq Publishing.

DayRay Literary Press is a literary imprint
of CCB Publishing: www.ccbpublishing.com

DayRay Literary Press
British Columbia, Canada
www.dayraypress.com

THE DAYS

OF THE

BITTER END

"So remember your Creator in the days of your youth, before the evil days come..."
- King Solomon

Praise received for *The Days of the Bitter End*

"It's all here...masterfully written by one of the greatest novelists of our Age. Engelhard puts the reader right in the center of the action...of the story...of the times. You will come away from this page-turner immersed not only in the Village scene, but especially in the background and events of the last day of the "Kennedy Years," a time when all of us privileged to be young were immersed in a New Spirit, a spirit we could all join in regardless of our politics. Engelhard brings to bear his journalistic talents as well as matchless storytelling ability to make those days of never to be seen again excitement come alive once more."
- John W. Cassell, author of *Crossroads: 1969*

"What a great story. If you missed the 60s – if you missed the excitement, the passion, the radicalism, the thrills, the hopes and dreams – this book brings it all alive. I could not put it down."
- Kmgroup review

"Another significant accomplishment from this versatile writer, and it resonates with the sort of dialogue and imagery that not only rings with credibility, but instantly evokes a 'you are there' feeling for the reader. An eye-popping cast of real-life characters mingle with Engelhard's well-crafted and multi-dimensional fictional ones, and one can't help but envision this being played out on the big screen."
- Nancy Sundstrom, *Northern Express*

"Engelhard's writing is superb, and he offers up a slice of 1960s life that is vibrant and moving. The story is skillfully crafted, quite witty and intriguing. The biggest lesson I found myself taking away from this book was that an era and the tragedy that defines that era can carry resounding effects for decades to come."
- Carie Morrison, *Rambles.net*

Also by Jack Engelhard

Indecent Proposal: Fiction.
Translated into more than 22 languages and turned into a Paramount motion picture of the same name starring Robert Redford and Demi Moore.

News Anchor Sweetheart: Fiction.

Compulsive: A Novel: Fiction.

Escape From Mount Moriah: Memoir.
Award-winner for writing and film.

Slot Attendant: A Novel about a Novelist: Fiction.

The Prince of Dice: Fiction.

The Bathsheba Deadline: Fiction.

The Girls of Cincinnati: Fiction.

The Horsemen: Non-fiction.
Excerpted in *The New York Times*

Writings: Commentary from Jack Engelhard the Voice of America's Conscience: Non-fiction.

* * * * *

A new Spanish language edition of *Indecent Proposal* will be released in 2013 in both print and e-book editions and made available for purchase worldwide.

For Leslie, my wife

Immeasurable gratitude to
Jeffrey Farkas, John W. Cassell, Linda Shelnutt

The author expresses his gratitude to Lois Sack for her devoted editorial assistance and inspirational support.

Deepest thanks and gratitude to editors Paul Rabinovitch, Nissan Ratslav Katz, Rochel Sylvetsky.

For historical signposts and sources, the author relied on William Manchester's brilliant *The Glory and the Dream* (Bantam Books) as his guide.

Chapter 1

Cliff Harris was thinking about Roberto, his barber, the man who had cut his hair only a short time ago. Roberto had come over from Milan six years back and still spoke no English, none that could be understood, and this was fine with Cliff. He needed no conversation getting his hair trimmed and styled and most times he needed no conversation at all if the talk was about his life as a fake Kennedy, which was mostly what it amounted to with tourists and strangers.

So Roberto only spoke Italian. Cliff did not know the language well, but he knew it well enough to guess what Roberto was saying to the barber at the next chair. What do you think will happen to this imposter, Roberto was saying earlier, if the real Kennedy gets killed?

Cliff could not be sure, otherwise he would have bolted from the chair - but it was a question that dogged him from all quarters. People wanted to know. They saw him, and they wondered; what would happen? It was as if people were *waiting*. Waiting for it to happen.

If it was meant as a joke, as it often was, Cliff failed to catch the humor. He hated the gig, but he loved Kennedy. Once in a while he even loved the gig, as it allowed him to clothe himself in the Kennedy magic - and to think that one day that magic might be snuffed out and be gone was staggering. The joke was too cruel, too gruesome for Cliff, and when he heard whispers he shuddered, not for himself, but for the country. Kennedy was America, and darn it, Cliff Harris was Kennedy, so bitch as he might, this trap he was in was not altogether bad. It was a living and it had its moments.

Cliff was in his uptown retreat making Kennedy faces in the mirror, something he regularly did as part of his rehearsal, and sometimes it took hours to get it down right. He was a perfectionist. Later he'd work on the voice and backstage he'd go over the mannerisms so that when he presented himself to the public the illusion would be complete. They'd get the entire package.

Today, however, even the face eluded him. Maybe it was the barber's remark that had him spooked, or maybe it was the fact that this prep was for a matinee and he was a night person, but in any case he was feeling jittery and the face wasn't coming. Nothing was.

It was his own fault, he figured, for agreeing to this afternoon gig. How much of it did he have to do to appease the throngs? Gloria MacKenzie, the club's manager, had talked him into it in terms of a patriotic duty. The people could not get enough of him and there weren't enough nights in the week. So he caved in, not for the extra money, nor for his patriotic duty, but for the chance to show his stuff to his friends, Ben, Richie, Louise and the others, and the material he had in mind for this special Friday afternoon was not Kennedy alone. No, he had a surprise in store. He had another routine, a departure from Kennedy, and this would be the time and the place to sample it, as an addition, and perhaps kick off a new career. There was another side to him, a real man with real talent behind the Kennedy mask. Lenny Bruce had also promised to be there "if I'm not behind bars, man."

Cliff longed for the approval of his peers, though, ironically, he kept an apartment uptown on East 72nd Street to remain chaste from the temptations of drugs, alcohol, and women. He availed himself only of alcohol and women. He was no skirt chaser. The skirts chased him. He was no alcoholic, either, but boozing was his only means to face the ogling multitudes without disdain. By nature he was reclusive anyway and while fame had caught up to him, he had not caught up to fame. This was intentional. He was afraid of growing bloated and corrupt.

He kept twisting the muscles of his face to achieve John Kennedy and was now panic-stricken. On this day, this afternoon, he would want to be at his best. On this day he would prove that he had not sold out to the Establishment. Lenny Bruce had made that accusation. Over at the Au Go Go a few nights back a lady got up to go to the bathroom. Lenny stopped mid-routine to heckle her. "Going across the street to catch that Government-approved phony?"

That stung, especially since Cliff counted on Lenny as a friend. Lenny later said it was just business.

Besides, Lenny said, what the fuck have you got to gripe about?

Perfectly true. Of the entire performing talent in the Village, and this included Odetta, Miriam Makeba, Richard Pryor, Bob Dylan, Peter, Paul and Mary, Woody Allen, Elaine May, Joan Rivers, the Highlight Singers, Bill Cosby, Tiny Tim, Flip Wilson, Barbra Streisand, Joan Baez, Judy Collins, of course Lenny Bruce, only Cliff Harris could claim absolute nationwide success, the devotion of millions coast to coast. He was a sensation, he was a phenomenon, he was the rage. (He's the human version of the hula hoop, Lenny Bruce quipped acidly, and perhaps enviously.)

Cliff Harris averaged four thousand letters a week praising his good looks and his pitch perfect rendition of JFK.

Cliff's agent, exasperated but pleased, was compelled to lease a special office and hire six secretaries just for the phone calls and the mail.

Good for the ego, but whose ego? Autograph seekers demanded that he sign Kennedy's name. When he declined, as always, he was often sneered at and cursed. Confusion was setting in as to what was real and what was illusion. The people were forgetting the joke.

During his mock press conferences from the stage of the Café Muse, earnest voices pressed him on Cuba, Russia, Vietnam, Bobby, but mostly Jackie. As if he really knew Jackie and as if he really had the answer for Fidel and the rising threat of communism. "Duck," he said when asked what America should do if Nikita Khrushchev dropped bombs along with his promise, "We will bury you." About the looming conflict in Vietnam, where American advisors were helping the corrupt South to stem the communist North, Cliff suggested a winner-take-all touch football game at the Kennedy compound at Martha's Vineyard "the way we Kennedys settle all our differences."

The people laughed at those snappy Kennedyesque one-liners. But now, late in 1963, with Republican Goldwater gaining in the polls as submitted by Gallup in today's November 22 *New York Herald Tribune*, they were still laughing, but not as much. They had come to expect real answers for real problems. Citizens, in trouble with IRS, irked by tardy Social Security checks, upset about everything from the military draft to late garbage pickup, were starting to demand action!

They came to him to complain. Wounded veterans wanted better hospitals. The elderly wanted improved medical care. The unemployed wanted better jobs and higher minimum wage; $1.25 an hour wasn't enough.

The joke was getting lost. The people thought they had elected him. They assumed that he had real powers. Guaranteed, once a night now a heckler would drunkenly denounce him as a fake, as if he pretended to be otherwise. Some disgruntled patrons demanded refunds when this surrogate of the president failed to satisfy them, or turned too flip - which is not to say that this was the rule. It was still the exception. But something was happening. The mood was changing.

Among the fan letters, beginning with bungled Bay of Pigs invasion of Cuba, there began to appear something sinister in the form of death threats. They were losing it all right, but so was he. On stage, John Kennedy was no longer part of his act, something he could drift into and out of, as in the beginning, back in 1961, when he'd *shpritz* Kennedy only between his normal routine as a stand-up.

Now, by popular demand, it was all Kennedy. He *was* John Kennedy. The haughty look, the aristocratic bearing, the New England vocal inflections, the athletic mannerisms, the rakish smile, all came so effortlessly that no one could be blamed for falling into a Kennedy trance, including the performer himself.

This was becoming Cliff's special terror. He was beginning to believe it himself. Even off-stage he caught himself thinking presidential thoughts. What *do* we do with the sonofabitch Castro? Is it time to send a CIA hit squad to go get Ho Chi Minh? Congress - Cliff reflected - is getting antsy about Vietnam. Why, they were beginning to ask, were those "advisors" dressed in Army uniforms, and why were more of them going in than coming out?

Cliff snapped out of such reveries just in time to reclaim his sanity, but he was getting lost in the myth, and to make public his disgust (mainly with himself) he began to booze openly.

Ed Sullivan, who admitted that he'd never seen an impressionist or any comedian or *any* performer capture the nation's fancy so wholeheartedly, took him aside one Sunday night, when Cliff had arrived inebriated for his 24th live appearance, to warn Cliff against such self-destructive behavior.

"You're killing it," Sullivan said. "If you don't shape up, don't come back." Moments later Sullivan introduced Cliff to his 68 million viewers with the usual riff: "And now, ladies and gentlemen, here he is, the President of the United States!" This was followed by Hail to the Chief.

Jack E. Leonard called Cliff a "prick" for defying success. Myron Cohen said, "With all the troubles in the world, *you're* complaining?" Jackie Gleason was fatherly: "Enjoy it while it lasts, son. These things don't go on forever. Take it from an expert."

Then there were the women. They were surprised that he wasn't tall (at five feet, ten inches he was three inches shorter than the president), that back here on earth, he wasn't lordly New England but rather lowly Philadelphia, that his normal speaking voice was raspy like sandpaper, that his demeanor was circumspect rather than outgoing - but still, they wanted him in bed, and they wanted him to do Kennedy in bed. They felt betrayed to discover otherwise. Where was the vigor! My gawd, said one martyr, you're only a *performer.*

Finally, now, the face was coming. Kennedy was materializing. But it wasn't his own face Cliff was worried about anymore. It was those other faces that would soon be coming at him in such expectation through the darkened theater. Such happy faces. Such a happy country, America. Was he the illusion? Or were they?

This much was real, Spencer's physics-turned-philosophy, force, counterforce. Or a time to live, a time to die. A time to laugh, a time to...

Ah, hell, he thought as he mugged one final time in the mirror, quit griping. Prick! You've been blessed. You've got the universe tilted in your favor. How many of your peers can say that! Like JFK himself, you have no equal. That's almost godly. THAT'S ALMOST GODLY!

There were still hours to go before showtime, so Cliff could relax, and he did so with a martini in front of the TV - and there he was, the real deal, on Cronkite's CBS, stepping off the plane in Dallas, Jack Kennedy, and Jackie, all smiles, those toothsome smiles that had lit up America and illuminated the entire world. Jackie was glorious (as usual) in her pink wool suit and pillbox hat. Jack was hatless and coatless and full of run. He sure had *vigah*, Cliff noted. As the Marines stood in arched attention along the runway, Texas Governor John B. Connally, Jr. stood waiting to greet the First Couple, "Welcome to Dallas," said the governor.

Chapter 2

Paul Hogan, Cliff's well-meaning manager and agent, a kindly gentleman, was on the phone to Cliff, asking if Cliff had caught Kennedy on TV just now, out there in Dallas. Yes he had. Well, Paul said, then you noticed that he hardly ever wears a coat, no matter how cold it is. Okay, said Cliff, catching Paul's drift.

"What I am saying," Paul went on, "is that for the sake of image, you shouldn't wear a coat, either."

"Never?"

"I mean out in public," Paul said submissively. He knew he was in trouble. Cliff could be difficult. Clients, they were all difficult, especially those that had shot up to stardom overnight. Cliff's problems were of a different sort, oddly enough that he disdained stardom - they were problems nonetheless. Besides all that, Cliff had a temper. An agent's job was to be supportive, but once in a while he had to be the bearer of bad news. A delicate task.

Cliff was disbelieving about this coat business. Agents!

"Paul, my man," he said, his powerful voice rising several decibels, "out in public I'm Cliff Harris."

"That's something we should discuss," Paul said timidly. "We're talking image."

"*You're* talking image. Paul, I've only got so many hours where I can be me. Those hours are precious."

"Well, I've heard grumbles."

"Like what?" Cliff said hotly.

"Now calm down, Cliff."

"Who's grumbling, Paul?" Cliff persisted.

"Ed Sullivan."

"Hot damn!"

"Just took a call from the man. Anyway, he thinks people have a certain expectation of you, around the clock. They see you like a regular guy out on the street and they're disappointed. He's heard from people who say it kills the illusion and even spoils what you do on stage. Only a suggestion, mind you, but I think you ought to give it some thought."

"Let me get this straight. You mean I can wear a coat, but only *inside* my own apartment!"

"Cliff, you're misunderstanding. Cut me some slack. I'm your front man for these people. I'm your pal."

"So we're not just talking about a coat."

"That image of Kennedy just now from Dallas, I guess that's what prompted Sullivan's call, I mean about your general appearance. No disrespect. Hey, Ed Sullivan loves you. I love you. We're talking about off-stage. Listen, Cliff, you've got a following, and you've got to respect that following. They expect a certain look from you."

"Dapper and dashing."

"Not that so much. Sullivan thinks you ought to be less rumpled. That was his word."

"Rumpled."

"Don't take it personal, Cliff. Y'know he means it for your own good. Me too. No offense, right? We're pals."

"Paul, do me a favor..."

"Cliff, we're pals, right?"

"Tell Sullivan to go fuck himself."

"Not again," Paul groaned.

Chapter 3

Of course Paul Hogan would do no such thing. Nobody told Ed Sullivan to go fuck himself. Ed Sullivan was the single most important man in television. Sunday nights America's streets were deserted because everybody was home watching *The Ed Sullivan Show*, which had begun as *The Toast of the Town* until Ed himself, a former gossip columnist, a poor man's Walter Winchell, got to be so big that they named the entire show after him and later an entire theater. He could make you, he could break you. He made the Beatles, even Elvis, and he broke Jackie Mason, plus countless others who were on once and never invited back again, only to slink forever into obscurity. So nobody told Ed Sullivan to go fuck himself. Nobody except Cliff Harris.

Cliff had two reasons for making the suggestion, going back to August. First, to make the point that he was a free man. Nobody was going to tell Cliff Harris (who was then flushed with excessive pride from his instantaneous and enormous success as Kennedy) whose show he could or could not be on.

Steve Allen - Sullivan's only rival - had extended the invitation and when Sullivan heard that Cliff was considering the offer from "that guy across the street," he went bonkers, and threatened to banish Cliff.

This led to Cliff's second motivation. To be banished from *The Ed Sullivan Show* and perhaps TV altogether would answer his death wish, that desire of his to be rid of the Kennedy gig and thus open the door to the real Cliff Harris.

So he told Ed Sullivan to go fuck himself. He said it to the man's face.

"What did you say?"

"Go fuck yourself."

"You're through, fella. You're done. You're gone. You're meat. Nobody uses that word on me."

"There's no other word for it," Cliff cracked.

"So fuck you, too."

Which was fine with Cliff, except for one thing. Cliff's agent, Paul Hogan, was likewise damaged by association, and was sure to go down the toilet along with his client. Paul, and his 28 other clients, were also dead.

Paul begged Sullivan for forgiveness, to no avail. For Paul's sake, Cliff was ready to make amends, but how? Over at the Hip Bagel among the usual gathering, Lenny Bruce had said, "Great career move, Cliff. You really needed that *fakakte* show for Mr. and Mrs. Fat Ass America? Latvian baton twirlers yet. Midgets on the harmonica. Let them all *gey kaken offen yam.* Good for you." Lenny paused and smiled to consider the quote. "Go fuck yourself. Wish I'd said that to the man. You've done us all proud, man."

"Ya had to be there," Cliff said chuckling.

"I was. I was with you in spirit."

But kidding aside, there had to be a way to get back into Sullivan's good graces out of fairness to Paul Hogan.

Ben said: "I still don't get it about pissing on fame and fortune. You said it to him twice?"

"Twice."

"Shit, Cliff, you don't even talk to us that way."

"That's because Cliff loves us," Richie piped in.

"That's right," said Howie.

"Shut up, Howie," everybody said.

"Here's the plan," said Ben. "We all go up together and tell the man Steve Allen threatened to kill you."

"That's ridiculous," said Richie.

"Wait a minute," said Cliff. "Go on, Ben."

"That's it," said Ben. "Steve Allen said he'd kill you if you don't do your gig on his show."

"Steve Allen?" said Richie. "He's as straight as they come."

"So we make up a story," said Lenny, warming to the scheme. "We tell Sullivan that Allen's got mob ties."

"Steve fucking Allen," said Richie. "Sullivan won't see through the deception?"

"Yeah," said Ben, "except that Sullivan hates the guy and will be ready to believe anything about him."

"Sounds good to me," said Cliff. "It's crazy enough to work."

Paul Hogan, pulling all strings, arranged the appointment and into Sullivan's office charged Ben, Richie and Cliff, and Louise Carmen, for the feminine touch. If nothing else clicked. Ben proceeded to explain how Steve Allen had been hounding Cliff, as naturally he would, America's most popular entertainer. When Cliff rebuffed him, time and time again, Steve Allen went to the muscle and had Cliff followed by two, make that four, thugs.

Ed Sullivan sat expressionless behind a big desk, all the while tapping a pencil to convey impatience and irritation. Or perhaps to convey nothing at all. His shoulders were slightly hunched over. He was a small man, almost frail, neither attractive or unattractive, not imposing or unimposing, certainly not glib, or witty, or even talented. All he had was power. An enormous amount of power. He had no expression on his face because he did not need an expression on his face and he had no talent because he needed no talent. All he needed was to be Ed fucking Sullivan.

"So, is that the whole story?"

"Yes," said Louise with all the perkiness she could muster on behalf of Cliff's career and Ben's rendition of events. Paul Hogan had not attended the meeting out of fear and wisdom.

"You expect me to believe that horseshit?" said Sullivan.

"No," said Cliff candidly.

"Listen," said Ben. "You just said horseshit. Cliff said fuck. Can we call it even?"

That was the best Ben could do. As it happened, Ed Sullivan wanted Cliff back anyway. He needed Cliff. The network needed Cliff. The nation needed Cliff. The only thing Sullivan wanted was some stroking, some groveling, some ass licking.

"We're even," Sullivan said getting up, smiling, and shaking hands all around.

For Cliff Harris he had these special words: "Welcome back, Mr. President. You asshole."

Chapter 4

Ben Jaffa had no legitimate reason to be where he was later in the morning, but for him it was legitimate enough to be standing in front of the Bitter End glaring across the street at Improv City, waiting for Jimmy Bleeds, who usually arrived at around this time with his big black dog. Ben was waiting with his fists clenched.

He had personal business with the man. Nothing at all to do with other business happening on Bleecker at the moment, like the sight of fuzz on horseback patrolling the street as though anticipating trouble. Spooky. Cliff's special matinee performance was not supposed to be that big a deal. Or was insurrection in the wind? Somebody must have tipped them off about something. Lenny again? Wasn't it time to arrest somebody else? Ben wondered. Maybe that was it, they were coming to arrest *everybody* in the Village for subversive speech - tirades from one end of the Village to the other against the "fat-cat" Establishment and police oppression. Lenny wasn't alone. Up and down, Bleecker heaved to the sounds of mockery. For the moment, this was none of Ben's business.

Normally, as the Bitter End's doorman and occasional bouncer, Ben did not show up until seven in the evening, arriving, casually but smartly in jeans and blue epaulet shirt open wide at the collar, just in time for the giggling young girls from Long Island who were usually first in line for

Cosby, and the first to cast admiring glances at this cool handsome doorman, who stood there like a prince.

Later, according to custom, when Bleecker Street started to sizzle, Fred Weintraub would show up and begin pacing outside the Bitter End. He owned the place. He was bearded and tall, standoffish, a head taller than the rest of the world, most visibly so when he stood there distractedly and stylishly puffing on a cigarette attached to an ivory cigarette-holder.

No one dared approach him - unless you were a suit from William Morris. That's what he was always waiting for anyway. As the probable discoverer of Peter, Paul and Mary, Bob Dylan, Joan Rivers, Bill Cosby, among a host of others, Fred certainly had had a hand in launching in the Sixties. The hootenanny was clearly his.

The folk singing craze sweeping the land - carrying with it protest ballads and an entire movement of discontent, discord and finally rebellion - most likely originated from this very spot.

The Bitter End was already a place of legend by the time Ben got there, and got the job, in late June. The cozy room with its Bohemian trappings was famed throughout the land. Fred Weintraub was known as the patient breeder of talent. He let then-struggling Bill Cosby room upstairs along his road to stardom, and it was said that from upstairs in the cold-water shelter Cosby took envious bows when he heard laughter coming from downstairs.

Tuesdays were hootenanny days at the Bitter End, amateur hour for country-faced young men and women arriving with banjos and guitars from all across America to wail against injustice. Set up against the famous red-brick backdrop that became stamped in America's consciousness by means of Peter, Paul and Mary's bestselling record album, the tyros got five minutes to make their case before the magisterial Fred Weintraub.

Most came and went. But wasn't it here on such a Tuesday that Bob Dylan was discovered? Likewise Peter, Paul and Mary? Wasn't it here that "If I Had a Hammer," "Puff the Magic Dragon," "Blowin' in the Wind" were first heard?

Fred Weintraub's Bitter End had become the hub of America's spawning subculture. Around it grew cabaret after cabaret as folk singing and blistering stream-of-conscious "improv" comedy became the rage. Up and down Bleecker deserted basements and abandoned storefronts were converted into coffeehouses featuring music and humor, all of it touched by a high-spirited iconoclasm, expressed freely and fervently as a summons to rise up against the rule of conformity and orthodoxy. Now was the moment to destroy America's sacred images. Ozzie and Harriet, as representative of family virtue, and any Rockefeller, as signifying Big Business, were to be scorned. A renaissance had broken out in the name of hipness. The big word was LOVE.

But love had nothing to do with Ben's self-motivated appointment. He only had to wait a few moments, and here came Jimmy Bleeds with his big black dog. The dog expressed itself with a menacing scowl and it was true, thought Ben, that people and their pets begin to look alike.

Ben watched as Jimmy Bleeds unlocked the front door to Improv City, the comedy store that Jimmy Bleeds owned and operated. He walked with a bully's fearless swagger. He was indeed a pock-faced two-fisted character, and undeniably Jacundo Belowj, as he was known to his parents when they brought him over from the Ukraine after the Second World War. Perhaps it was true that he and his parents had been friends of the Nazis and had helped the Gestapo. Perhaps it wasn't true.

That wasn't the point.

"Hey, Jimmy," Ben called out, a lump in his throat. He remembered what his sister had said about everything being for the best, but he also had to keep reminding himself that he was a Black Belt.

Find the good in everything, she had also said. Now there was a mountain. Find the good in people, all people. Now there was Mt. Everest. "Hey, Jimmy. Jimmy Bleeds."

But Jimmy Bleeds had already slammed the door shut. Ben went knocking on the door.

"Open up."

"What do you want?" came the husky voice.

"You know what I want."

Ben wanted justice. True, Ben Jaffa was not yet focused on a career and yes it was the Village joke that he was not only between careers but also between lives, and indeed his aimlessness was a source of pride - he was too noble to pursue a career - but yet he did have something in the works.

Ben Jaffa, perceiving himself a budding writer - and in the Village any man bereft of a profession was a "writer" - had written a sketch that showed how easy it was to dupe the press and the public.

Giorgos Seferis of Greece had recently been awarded the 1963 Nobel Prize in Literature. "Who?" was the unanimous response among the uninitiated, which included just about everybody. Nobody, at least in this country, knew the guy. But the *Times* here and the *Times* there found the one and only Seferis scholar in America whose report gushed with superlatives. Giorgos Who was indeed worthy, and perhaps the greatest writer of our age. The press bought it - hook, line and stinker, as Ben said - and so did the public. If only for one day.

The newspapers ran excerpts from Giorgos Who's best work, which was mostly nonsense and gibberish - but fawned over by the literary elite. Why? Because intellectuals were lemmings who followed the leader.

Because if one rabbi said it was kosher, all rabbis said it was kosher - and that was the crux of Ben's takeoff which he had written as a play and worked wonderfully as a skit. He had presented the material to Jimmy Bleeds back in September. Jimmy said he'd think about it and now it was November and Ben's play was a hit.

It was even reviewed favorably in *The New Yorker*, *The New York Times* and the *Village Voice*. But without Ben's name as the creator. Due to an oversight, as Ben chose to believe, Jimmy Bleeds had forgotten to give credit where credit was due, and that was all Ben was demanding, his name, nothing more than his name attached to his work. As it was, the skit went on without naming an author of any sort. Forget the money, Ben said to Jimmy Bleeds as September became October. Just put my name up. That goes for the marquee and the program.

At the outset, Jimmy Bleeds had professed innocence. Theatrically slapping a palm to his forehead, he exclaimed, "How did this happen? My mistake. I'm sorry. Tomorrow I'll get it all straightened out. Tomorrow."

That never happened, and the topper came now in November, when just yesterday, Thursday, Jimmy Bleeds announced himself the author. That was it for Ben. Until then Ben had been more or less resigned. Indeed, Richie had said, "Why so apathetic? You afraid of him or something? The sonofabitch stole your work!" Cliff Harris had been even more emphatic. Cliff knew the value of a labor of love and he was pained for Ben. "I'd kill the motherfucker," Cliff had said.

That was even before Jimmy Bleeds took the final step of naming himself the author of Ben's work.

Ben had not really been apathetic throughout the ordeal; he had merely been keeping in step to the drumbeat of the Village. This was not the place for confrontation. This was the place where gentle, bearded poets read their stuff to enthralled cider-sipping hipsters and tourists at the San Remo Bar, people snapping their fingers rather than clapping their hands in appreciation. This was the place where Irwin Shaw and James Jones played chess outside the Café Feenjon. This was the place where young men and women sang... "It's the hammer of justice, it's the bell of freedom; it's the song about love between my brothers and my sisters all over this land."

Vengeance was out of season until today.

"What can I do for you?" Jimmy Bleeds demanded after unbolting the door.

Ben told him, but deferentially. People read something then they forget who wrote it - happens all the time.

"I'm willing to give you the benefit of the doubt."

Jimmy Bleeds was all chest and bull-neck, eyes bulging. He had the broad full-face of a peasant, its complexion raw.

"You're a bigger fool than I thought," he laughed.

"You mean you admit you stole, you plagiarized?"

"Stole? Fuck you. I didn't steal. I borrowed. Everybody does that. It's called *homage*. Grow up, boy."

"Fuck the homage. Gimme my name."

"Fuck your name."

That guy Cliff Harris, said Jimmy Bleeds, what was he doing if not homage? What about those other Kennedy impersonators around the country? Were they all ripping off Cliff Harris? Wasn't Cliff Harris himself ripping off John

Kennedy? Call it that or call it homage. Call it a compliment. That's what it was, a compliment. Otherwise, fuck you.

I swear, said Jimmy Bleeds, just watching Kennedy arriving in Dallas this morning, watching him on the TV, I swear for a second I thought it was Cliff Harris. I thought it was Cliff Harris in Dallas. That's how blurred the whole thing's become. That's a compliment to Cliff. That's what I call homage. Yeah.

Jimmy Bleeds went on to say that ideas were public domain. Ideas were in the air, meant to be plucked. In fact, the Nobel Prize idea had been his all along, he simply had not refined it, busy as he was running a club and having to deal with actors who had to *rehearse* their improvisations, actors who were nothing more than children, needing to be babied all the time - so fucking insecure. So, he simply had not put it down on paper, was all. Ben Jaffa had done that for him. Thank you very much.

Ben, forgetting himself - forgetting that this was not the season - raised a Black Belt arm.

"Touch me and you're a dead man."

There was that, too. Jimmy Bleeds was rumored to be connected.

"This isn't over," Ben said.

"I'll be waiting," Jimmy Bleeds said.

Chapter 5

On this Friday, November 22, 1963, Patrolman Rick Ornstein had the 8 to 4 tour. Working out of Greenwich Village's Sixth Precinct - which encompassed the south side of 14th Street to the north side of Houston Street, and from the west side of Broadway all the way to the West Side Highway - Ornstein was on the alert for something unusual, unusual enough to spook him.

Most briefings for Sector Boy, the "Glass Post," so called because so much of it was Bleecker's storefronts, concerned break-ins, stolen cars, public intoxication, fights, drugs, and runaways. Greenwich Village was runaway haven and Ornstein, storied for his compassion, was known as "King of the Runaways" for his skill at tracking them down and returning them to their homes.

This morning, however, the alarm was out for a possible assassin. The tip had come from an anonymous caller who warned that someone was out to get a particular club performer. Clearly, the suspect was an individual who did not like the president or his impersonators. In this morning's briefing, Sgt. Louis Packwood had announced:

"We have received an anonymous tip that a possible assassin will be trying to get a comedian who imitates the President of the United States."

This could only be Cliff Harris. That realization chilled Ornstein, as it could be the precursor to something larger.

From experience he knew how these things went, in trends. When it was quiet, all was quiet. First a single burglary, then a series. Assassin was not a word he liked to hear.

Rick Ornstein, though only 24, knew his beat inside and out. He knew practically everybody and virtually everything that was going on. He even knew that a disturbance was taking place inside Improv City and that Ben Jaffa was involved, but not involved enough for police action. Ornstein was aware of Ben's particular problem with Jimmy Bleeds, but he could only give advice, which was, "Stay cool, and stay in shape. If you know what I mean." Ornstein was known as "Super Jew" because of his weightlifting prowess, so his friendship with Black Belt Ben Jaffa was only natural.

Ornstein loved the Village. He was stimulated by the clashing cultures, the jazz clubs, the rock clubs, even the gay bars and the turbulence of mutiny that was afoot; certainly the art galleries, the terrific restaurants from Chinese to Italian and everything in between, and he had a special fondness for the nurses at St. Vincent Hospital.

He loved the ferment and the hot and cool bongo-drum rhythm of the place and it can even be said that the place loved him back. If any cop could be said to be on friendly terms with the hip, it was Ornstein. He belonged to the generation, the only difference being he wore a uniform.

Even those who loathed the fuzz understood (to an extent) that when it was time to raid a gay bar, it was simply Ornstein enforcing the Law. (Though it was mostly the Law that the radicals were protesting against.)

Such raids were not Ornstein's favorite part of the job, and neither was it pleasant for him to be among New York's finest to raid the Café Au Go Go and march out Lenny Bruce in handcuffs, to the sound jeers.

This was not what Ornstein was all about, but it was his job.

Ornstein - a member of the policeman's Hebraic *Shom-rim* Society - was one of four Jewish cops attached to the Sixth Precinct, the rest mostly Irish and Italian, and he'd been brought up on the proposition of "live and let live."

So he was Jewish, but he was a cop, not that the two necessarily conflicted, as Judaism was all about Laws; at the same time, though, it was also a faith that called for tolerance and loving your fellow man.

Somehow, Ornstein had managed to find contentment between the extremes; the severity of Law against the ideal of mercy.

In fact, his reason for becoming an officer was based on the Biblical injunction to love the good and hate evil, and also upon the comic book imperative to "help people and fight crime."

Such motivation was an anachronism for the Sixties, but Ornstein was a child of the Fifties. On the lower east side of Manhattan in Alphabet City, Avenue D, he grew up with a father who adhered to the Ten Commandments, which he called mental toughness, but also believed in boxing, which he called physical toughness, and though his dad was a house painter by trade, boxing was his true profession, so it came as no surprise that Ornstein's brother would become a heavyweight world champion wrestler known as Jack "Wild Man" Armstrong and that, after Seward Park High School on Delancey and tryouts with Dodgers and Yankees, and years of bodybuilding to impress his father, Ornstein would attend John Jay College for studies in Police Science and go on to become a real live cop.

As opposed to Fort Apache the Bronx, Fort Bruce, Greenwich Village, was about as crime-free as it could get in New York. Murder was rare in the Village; assassination unheard of and unknown.

Yes, the feds came in now and again to monitor Lenny and Cliff and some others, but only to check on subversive material like the *Seven Forbidden Words* and not to stop any possible assassination. This was new, and suggested the kind of peril decidedly outsized for the Sixth Precinct.

The description of the suspect was light-haired Caucasian male, 5'8", 185 pounds, wears motorcycle jacket, has tattoos, a scar on left cheek, brown eyes and was seen with a bleached blonde who resembles Marilyn Monroe.

The last item drew hoots and whistles during the assignment, but Ornstein, now on foot patrol but in contact with his partner by walkie-talkie, knew the gravity of the situation. It added up that if someone was out to get the imposter, someone else, perhaps in a coordinated attempt, perhaps not, was out to get the genuine article. Specifically, Ornstein reasoned, if someone hated Cliff Harris, Cliff being but a reflection of the true president, imagine how much more the president himself was at risk.

At the Big Fat Black Pussy Cat on Minetta Lane, Ornstein went off foot patrol and hooked up with his partner, Patrolman Ken Massaria, who would be driving squad car RMP 346 as Ornstein worked the recorder seat while they made the usual rounds. Massaria and Ornstein had been rookie cops together. In their gray Police Academy rookie uniforms, they had started off patrolling Times Square and they still spoke about the time someone rushed up to Massaria, who was merely directing traffic at Port Authority, to voluntarily give himself up. The man held out his arms ready to be shackled. To the amazement of the brass, the guy turned out to be among the Ten Most Wanted.

Speaking of today's alarm, Massaria said the tip may have been bogus, a hoax. Ornstein, toughened by a year's duty in the Bronx, said he was inclined to believe otherwise.

"You actually think someone's out to kill a *comedian*?" Massaria laughed.

"This in no ordinary comedian."

"Yeah," Massaria had to agree, "and these aren't ordinary times."

As if to underscore that observation, some longhaired radical yelled out "Pig" as, now on Cabaret Patrol, they cruised past Trudy Heller's on Ninth. Ornstein and Massaria pretended not to hear it - but it stung.

Sometimes even the extra coat of thick skin was insufficient cover against those slings and arrows. Ornstein knew what was going on, but he did not always understand. The *Seven Dirty Words* were coming out of the closet as, at the same time, the term Law and Order was being denounced as reactionary. Militancy was in the air, revolution was in the wind. The Black Panthers, the Weathermen, and the Hispanic FALN group were emerging from out of the mist of discontent. Black Power was beginning to turn from a whisper to a shout. Abby Hoffman and Jerry Rubin were gaining fame as hecklers of the System. Ornstein, as an almost-seasoned cop and still a young man, was prepared to listen as long as chaos wasn't being offered as an alternative. Meanwhile, despite being the object of some loathing for his uniform and derision for his badge, he felt no resentment, only puzzlement. He loved America and it vexed him that the country had taken up sides.

You were hip or you were square; you were radical or you were Establishment. The frontlines of this still-verbal warfare was Greenwich Village itself where Lenny Bruce and Jack Kerouac served the spearcarriers against conformity, each in his own way drawing converts for the oncoming conflict against Authority. Which in a word meant the fuzz. They, the cops, were the face of Authority, the shock troops of the Establishment. All of this was quite highfallutin to Ornstein. He was just a guy doing a job.

As they wheeled past the Café Rienzi on MacDougal, they saw a bumper sticker on a Caddy, obviously from uptown, that read: *Need help? Call a Hippie!* The backlash was already setting in even as the revolution was still merely an upheaval.

In silence they cruised the beat in zigzag fashion on the lookout for the usual but on alert for a particular suspect. Their patrol took them around Washington Square Park, to the fire house on Third, to the campus at NYU, to the houses at LaGuardia Place, to the Eighth Wonder on Eighth, to the Village Barn along the same stretch, then to the Bon Soir where the girl making a name for herself was Streisand, to Dirty Dick's off West Side Highway, to the Village Vanguard on Seventh Avenue and Ninth Street, where Tiny Tim was tiptoeing through the tulips, then to the Blue Note on Third, where they stopped to shoo away a group of panhandlers who were beginning their invasion from the Third Street Shelter in the Bowery.

At Whelan's Drugs, on the corner of Eighth Street and Sixth Avenue, they stopped in for smokes. At the Hip Bagel they stopped in for coffee and a bagel. At St. Vincent's Hospital, on Seventh Avenue and Tenth Street, they gave the duty clerk a description of the suspect.

Back in their radio motor patrol they noticed that someone had shot out the outside lights at the Village Gate, and they called it in. Chess boards were being set up at the Café Feenjon back on Bleecker. Lunch was being served at the Kettle of Fish across from the Bitter End. Next door the Bleecker Street Cinema was showing Truffaut's *400 Blows.* (That's where both Ornstein and Ben Jaffa came to cool off after hours.) A few doorways down at the Café Au Go Go a sign said that Lenny Bruce's performance had been cancelled for the weekend by order of the police. Chairs and tables were being dusted off at the Café Figaro. Published and unpublished writers were getting an early start on sandwiches and booze at the Lion's Head on Christopher Street off Seventh Avenue. Back on Bleecker they found the doors to Elaine May's Premise Theatre unlocked but no signs of a break-in.

At the Premise Theatre, also known as the Third Eye, that's where the improv boys and girls needled the Establishment and the cops without pity, especially after a raid on Lenny Bruce.

If the raid at the nearby Au Go Go took place in the early evening, by late evening there'd be a skit ready at the Premise mocking the cops and reenacting the raid to wild applause.

Ornstein, his partner noticed, was not his chipper self this day.

"Really bugged about that alarm, huh?"

"Let's try the shit houses."

The Village Hotel on Bleecker was a dumping ground for bums prone to violence, as was the Jane West Hotel on Jane Street and West Side Highway, but today, nothing out of the ordinary. "The usual suspects," cracked Massaria.

Ornstein felt that maybe they were trying too hard. Sometimes it fell on your lap when you were looking the other way. Just as it happened to Massaria in Times Square. So upon Ornstein's urging they made a pizza stop at Arturo's on Houston, which drew the artsy crowd and today found Joe Franklin, the fabled host of WOR radio and TV, seated at a table with Paul Newman, Woody Allen, Dustin Hoffman and Al Pacino.

Franklin offered a pleasant nod to the two officers and Ornstein was moved to complete the exchange by noting, "There's the real Ed Sullivan," as it was both inside information and common knowledge that Joe Franklin had jump-started the careers of Elvis and Barbra and a host of others even before Ed Sullivan got his hands on them. It was said that the road to stardom was paved through the avenue of Joe Franklin.

At John's Pizza on Bleecker uptown tourists were elbow to elbow. But still, nothing close to the man and woman on their alarm. At the Dugout next door to the Bitter End they stepped down for another cup of coffee and were hailed by Bernie Schwartz. "How's the Superjew?" said Bernie otherwise known as Tony Curtis.

"Making the rounds," said Ornstein, feigning nonchalance.

"Anything special?"

"Nah. The usual. Need help making a movie?"

"If it's about cops, I'll know who to call for advice," said the famous movie star with a laugh and a wink. Though of different generations, Ornstein and Bernie Schwartz were both graduated from Seward Park High School on Grand Street in Manhattan.

Next stop was the Sheridan Square Health Club where both gays and straights worked out together. No luck here, either, though Ornstein agreed to be back later to spar a couple of rounds with Rocky Graziano.

"Let's try the park again," Ornstein suggested.

They circled the Square. Allen Ginsberg was railing against the Establishment and beginning to draw a crowd of weekend hippies. Some artists were setting up their easels and others were already painting the scene.

"Uh-oh," said Massaria.

"Let's go," said Ornstein.

What caught their attention was a blue Impala moving erratically. They stopped the car and when the driver got out Ornstein and Massaria exchanged a knowing glance.

This could be the suspect. He fit the description. So did his blonde companion.

Ornstein opened with a casual conversation. What are you doing here, where are you from, where are you going? "Doing nothing and going nowhere, it's a free country," came the response, but Ornstein had already detected the smell of liquor on the man's breath, so that at the very least there was now cause to book him on a DWI, a Deewee, driving while intoxicated.

"Mind if we search your car?" Massaria asked.

"Fuck you."

Ornstein was already inside the vehicle. In it he found a bag of marijuana, a pair of handcuffs, a loaded .38 caliber Smith and Wesson, newspaper clippings of John F. Kennedy and two copies of Cliff Harris' record album "Thank You, Mr. President."

"I'm a fan," the punk brashly protested with a smirk while shifting nervously on his feet and glancing around as if to make a run.

"Some fan," Massaria said as he secured the loaded pistol in his own gunbelt.

"Hey, what have I done?"

"Nothing yet," said Ornstein. "Just to be sure, please come along with us."

Ornstein called in to have the Impala impounded as he a Massaria brought them both to the Sixth Precinct at 135 Charles Street, handcuffed on charges of intoxication and possession of a loaded weapon and drugs. Evidence of an attempt to assassinate would require further investigation.

For now, there was enough to put them both behind bars. The blonde went along willingly, but the punk kept up a chatter about this being a free country.

Later, back on patrol, Massaria said, "Think we stopped something?"

"Maybe."
"Something big?"
Ornstein shrugged that Yiddish shrug of foreboding.

Chapter 6

After bolting from Louise Carmen and still smoldering from her announcement that she'd soon be off to bed with her old boyfriend Roger in Wheeling, Richie Bell fled to Gloria MacKenzie for comfort. Gloria lived in a loft up on Sullivan where it met Bleecker.

"No guitar?" she said, amazed and amused.

"No guitar," he said sullenly.

She shrugged and arched an eyebrow as if to say it was none of her business, but of course it was. Everything was her business, everything around the Village and certainly everything that had to do with Richie Bell, the current man in her life, whether he liked it or not.

"What the fuck happened?"

"Louise Carmen."

"Of course," she drawled wisely. "Who else would it be? So what happened?"

"It's a long story."

"I've got time."

"I broke it," he said.

"The guitar that you love more than anything in the world?" she tweaked. "Next to Louise Carmen. That guitar?"

"That guitar."

"What the hell did she do, our precious Miss Carmen?"

Richie knew that telling her would only give her satisfaction, so he decided to put it off for as long as he could, though in the end he'd tell, have to tell, because Gloria Mac-Kenzie owned a certain part of him, old as she was.

No not old, but definitely older and beyond her prime.

Gloria, who managed the Café Muse, was in her early 50's and despite a face that looked a bit chopped up and a voice filled with years of gin and tobacco and eyes that were always bloodshot, all was not hopeless. She had a certain something about her, call it wisdom, even call it sexiness that comes with age. Among her charms was her open self-loathing. I am the ugliest woman in the world, she liked to say, and appeasing her, flattering her, sometimes consumed an entire night, even an entire friendship.

She was not ugly, merely tired. She had been around. She had loved too much. She had hated too much. She had traveled too far. She had stayed in one place too long, namely the Village.

She had hurt too many. She had been hurt too often. She had read every book, seen every movie, heard every song. She knew all the jokes. There were mysteries left, but no surprises.

She was simply tired.

She had endured three awful marriages, and there were even children, somewhere. She did not know where. Anyway, they were well past college age and could take care of themselves. Some may even have gotten married.

Better to forget, forget everything. That's why she'd come to the Village in the first place so many years ago. To forget and start all over. Indeed, as manager of the Café Muse and the star maker to Cliff Harris, the biggest show in town *and* the nation, she was a success, but strictly in the business sense of the word.

When it came to men, that's where it got touchy. She'd been bounced around and brutalized time and again and had finally sworn off the opposite sex, until Richie Bell came along with his silken voice, tussled brown hair, confident stride and mischievous gleam in his eye. She got hooked. More than twice his age, but hooked.

Actually, she made a public fool of herself.

She kept forgetting that Richie was all about fun and that nothing (besides Louise Carmen) could tie him down, so it was ridiculous of her to insist that he stay with her, forever. Marry me, she kept saying, until it became a joke, another Village joke, and she, Gloria MacKenzie, had no choice but to laugh along, otherwise the joke would be on her.

Fun, that was Richie from beginning to end, meaning that when he laughed her off he was not intending to be cruel. Fun was why he came to the Village. Fun was why he played with snakes and toyed with squares from Cleveland over at the Hip Bagel. (All tourists and squares were from "Cleveland.") He was in it for laughs.

She knew that Richie was just using her. She had power. Certainly in the Village. Even uptown she pulled some weight. She knew Ed Sullivan and Joe Franklin. She could make him a star. He'd even ask her why she was so reluctant to give him a shot at the Café Muse as maybe an opener for Cliff Harris.

You're not ready, she'd say. But if that's all you want out of me, she'd pout, why hang around? He'd give her that laugh and say, "You're good company, that's why."

That she was. She could talk endlessly about books, art, literature, music, and politics, chain-smoking from one topic to the next. She was stimulating. That was one reason why Richie cleaved to her. The other reason was that, although he took her to bed, she was a mother-figure. She did not mind that, playing Gertrude Stein to his Ernest Hemingway. What she did mind was that he came running to her only when he was in trouble. She had become a place to go and hide, a place to stay and stave off the real world. She was a place. In the end, Louise Carmen would have him.

Gloria hated Louise Carmen, but not so much as an individual as much as a type. So pristine and virginal, as they all were when they came from the sticks, but only to get fucked, that's why they came to Greenwich Village, to get fucked and go back as virgins.

She hated that type for a more compelling reason. She had once been them. She had once been 18, too. *Now look.*

Only with Richie Bell was she 18 again. Except when he sang that awful ditty about "the girl that I marry." That drove her through the roof, and that made him sing it even more often. Not being cruel, just having fun.

Here was a man in his prime. In this Bohemian semi-decadent setting of Greenwich Village, Richie thrived. Back home in Connecticut he'd been a most obedient son. His life as the perfect citizen (along the Platonic ideal) had been charted out even before he was born by loving but domineering parents who had him programmed from cradle to grave. He would be beautiful, and he was. He would be brilliant, and he was. Straight A's. He would marry well. So far he had not, though there was the girl back home and she was waiting. He would follow his father as a lawyer. Not yet. But he was more than halfway there. The other half, for the moment, belonged to Greenwich Village and Louise Carmen.

For him too, as for Ben Jaffa, it had all begun as a summertime diversion. Most well-to-do students from New England families misspent their summers in Florida and California. He chose Greenwich Village because he had a guitar and a flair for music. (Or so he had thought.)

Also, there was a rebellion of sorts going on, and he wanted in on the action. He was tired of being a conventionally spoiled child. Back in Connecticut it had been the usual stuff. Skipping classes (only now and then), whoring (a regular upstairs at Freddie's Pool Hall), gambling (same place), dating (everyone in sight, with a particular eye for waitresses), spending too much on clothes, (to accentuate his God-given looks) - but where the conventional gave way to the bizarre was his love of snakes. No cobra of his had ever done harm - but there was always that menace. Maybe he wasn't the safe suburban rich kid everyone assumed him to be.

Maybe it was his way of telling the world that there was nothing serious enough to hold him down.

But then along came Louise Carmen to turn him into her slave. She had commanded him to quit smoking, and he did. Drinking? Likewise. She approved of no friendship with strange women - this same woman who juggled Richie along with Ben and Roger/Rasputin back in Wheeling - but here he balked, but only to make her jealous.

Sometimes it worked.

Louise was even jealous of his relationship with Gloria MacKenzie. This surprised Richie and amused Gloria.

Now, when he finally confided to Gloria the reason behind his misery, Gloria said:

"I hate to say I told you so. But I did tell you she's flighty and too full of herself to stick to one guy."

"You mean she doesn't love me?"

"No, I mean she's a woman who has choices, and a woman with choices is very dangerous. You're learning."

That he was. For Richie, too, this was a time of decision. It was November for him as it was November for Ben. The summer of '63 was over and gone. He could not help but notice how the streets of the Village were getting emptier by the day.

People were moving on. Cliff Harris would soon be departing, going on a tour of his own. Ben - how long would he last? It was day-to-day with Ben. Even the Village Gate

35

where he, Richie, waited tables was growing tattered and weary. Richard Pryor had become a hit and was moving on. At the Bitter End, Bill Cosby had become so embraced by uptown that the Village would soon be old hat. He was surely going to television. Woody Allen was back and forth from Hollywood.

Even the crowds weren't the same. Those happy young faces, cruising Bleecker in their shiny Sting Rays, were becoming less and less visible while the dregs from the Bowery seemed to be growing more and more prominent.

All of this bespoke an end. Nothing permanent for there would always be next summer. But for now, it was finished. There was nothing left to do. So what was he doing here, still hanging around? Waiting to make it as a folk singing star, that was one excuse. Louise Carmen, that was the real reason.

And Louise Carmen was leaving! She was coming back, in two weeks she said, but next time, next tour, she'd be gone for good, because as for the Highlight Singers, they too were in demand nationally. Ballads were the national craze. Louise had been hinting about a weekly TV show from Hollywood modeled after Fred Weintraub's *Hootenanny*. Wasn't he happy for her? she demanded. Yes he was. Sure he was. Sure. Wouldn't he be glad to come along and join her out there? Of course he would. Like any good puppy.

Of his own career as a folksinger, with dreams to rival Bob Dylan, this much was clear: No!

"You haven't failed," Gloria insisted as he poured on the self-pity.

Gloria was fearful, as always, that he'd face the truth about his talent and abandon the Village. Abandon her. A part-time Richie was still Richie and she feared for the emptiness of her life without him.

The truth was that Richie had talent, but so did a million others. He had looks and stage presence, which could not be counted in the millions, especially not stage presence, but it could be counted in the thousands.

With his olive complexion, curly black hair, sometimes brooding, sometimes playful eyes he had no trouble holding a living room audience. He sang beautifully and he strummed the guitar soulfully.

But he was not *unique*. Not on stage.

"A career takes time," Gloria said. "It takes years. Look how long it took Fred to groom Cosby. What have you given? Months?"

In that time he had auditioned up and down the strip and along the side streets. Though not needing the money, he had even passed around the hat Bob Dylan-style at the San Remo. The quarters failed to come. Something was lost between Richie's living room performances and the clubs. He failed to touch people. Maybe, Gloria thought, it was because he had never felt any real pain - that's what was missing pain and suffering. He had yet to be soiled by adversity. But she'd never tell him. She did not want him to lose his extraordinary gift of joy. Pain and suffering, let the others know it and wail about it, but let Richie go free. That's how she loved him, unfettered and unstained.

But now, why so sad?

There was a party coming up in a few hours right after Cliff Harris' matinee and Richie loved parties. Enter Richie and the party begins. Exit Richie and the party ends. Richie's presence was required for any happening to be worthy of the name.

"I'll be there for Cliff. I don't know about the party," Richie said.

"Stop that sulking, you big baby. Your girl hasn't left yet - and you always have me."

"Thanks," Richie said with a chuckle. "That's good to know."

"How good?"

This she said with a smile, but it was a smile waged with tears. He stroked her hair and she began to violently undress him. During the lovemaking she was not making love but holding on for dear life. It was all coming apart. There would be no more parties and soon there would be no more Richie. Everybody was leaving. It happened every fall. It began every summer and it ended every fall.

Chapter 7

It was getting close to noon, but not too early for Cliff Harris to saunter over to Smitty's Saloon and Eatery on Second Avenue to get himself lubricated in advance of his matinee special opening in about an hour. Cliff downed three whiskies, straight, and gazed around the joint. Usual crowd. Because of his fame and resemblance to JFK most public places were out of bounds for Cliff, especially so when he had his hair combed Kennedy-style. That made him a dead ringer and too often an object of sport. Cliff hated to be recognized out on the street and he hated to be hassled, as was beginning to happen more and more often. "Hey, tell us about your new *fronteah*, Mr. fuck-up president!"

Like that. That was being hassled and it was coming from the other end of the bar from some beer-soaked character who wasn't a regular at Smitty's but was around now and then and whose mild joshing in the past had been only slightly irritating. Big Nick was his name and he always seemed to have a political gripe.

Cliff grinned. The most he would say, as Big Nick kept up his patter, was: "Politics ain't my bag."

"Not so's I can tell," said Big Nick, now shouldering his way over to Cliff's stool.

"Hey, chill," said Cliff, still grinning. "Peace."

"Fuck peace. Fuck Kennedy. Fuck you."

"I'm just making a living, man. Come on."

"You like that fucking bird up in the White House? He's your man, right? Hey, you're his man. Look at you!"

With that, Big Nick took the liberty. He ran his fingers through Cliff's hair mussing it all up and turning it into a mop. That was the end for Cliff. Touch anything, but never the hair after it had been so artistically (and expensively) groomed Kennedy. On impulse from his years as a kid on the streets of Philadelphia, Cliff wheeled around and landed a backhand to the guy's nose. Stu the bartender ran around and stepped between the two as Cliff was ready for more. Big Nick tried to stand his ground but the blood kept flowing and finally he ran off to the john.

"You had cause," Stu assured Cliff, "but better you should take a walk."

Cliff took a walk but could not seem to cool down. He walked with his fists clenched, his face flushed in rage. What a world! It was the public he detested. All kinds of people out there, he was now thinking - for what? His burly chest heaved in indignation. He had boxed as a young man in Philadelphia and today he was ready for more. Lately he was always ready for more.

True, as he had told the bully, politics was not his bag but it was a burden he had to live with as a Kennedy impersonator. He was such an easy target for anyone who had a grudge against the president, and surprisingly, so many people did. Cliff was chilled by the fact that out there, there existed another America, a Nixon America, a McCarthy America. Kennedy had beaten Nixon by the slimmest margin in the nation's history, so they were out there all right, simmering in their wine of bitterness and waiting their turn. That was the America that Cliff feared would one day rise up and it was no idle threat; it was no secret that once or twice he had overdosed purposely on sleeping pills, to the terror of both his personal manager Paul Hogan and his manager at the Café Muse, Gloria MacKenzie.

They had a big stake in Cliff Harris. His boozing was one thing, but the disrespect he had for his own life was cause for anxiety.

But that was Cliff's nightmare; that at any moment the brightness of Kennedy would be eclipsed by the looming shadow of the red-necked Philistines. Big Nick wasn't alone. There were millions of them.

Yes, he was only an entertainer, a comedian at that, but obviously he was much more. If the adoring multitudes had taken Cliff Harris to their hearts as the president incarnate, who could blame the hatemongers for making the same mistake - and there was no mistaking that the president, the most popular man in the world, was also the most unpopular man in the world.

To the left, he was moving too slowly on civil rights. To the right, he was moving too fast. On disarmament, conservation, rebuilding the slums, Vietnam, Russia, Cuba, he had made friends and foes. Shortly, his New Fronteah would be coming up against the hawkish and conservative Barry Goldwater, but some activists wanted things changed even before next year's elections.

Kennedy was viewed by his adversaries as too cosmopolitan, too European, too much to the left along the lines of Willy Brandt in Germany, Harold Wilson in Britain and Pietro Nenni in Italy. He was glamorous and glorious all right - he and Jackie were - but insufficiently *American*. His wife seemed better at French than at English. She seemed more at home in Paris than in Washington. (Even this morning, only about an hour ago in Dallas before the cheering throngs, Kennedy cracked that he was the man who had merely accompanied Jackie to Paris, just as he was the man who was now accompanying Jackie to Texas.)

When John Kennedy proclaimed "Ich Bin Ein Berliner" not everyone cheered. When he allowed Khrushchev to put up the Berlin Wall virtually overnight, there was no singing and dancing in the West. When he failed to finish something that he had started, namely the bungled Bay of Pigs invasion into Cuba, his opponents, who had been waiting for just such a misstep from a president too young and too Catholic, turned grim.

Even the Cuban missile stand-off, at which Kennedy emerged at least in a dead heat with Khrushchev, alarmed many Americans for the brinksmanship that was required. (Never would have gotten that close with Eisenhower, people said.)

All that bread of affliction was Cliff's to share. Along with the fan letters there was hate mail. In too many instances, especially after the Bay of Pigs and after the Berlin Wall, there were death threats.

These were growing more frequent and more sinister as Kennedy moved from his first year in office, to the second, and now the third. This news was kept from the public. But as the putative John Kennedy, Cliff knew things no one else knew. He knew things only the real John Kennedy knew. The letters, the good and the bad, bound them together and did indeed make them joined at the hip. So there was that other America out there for both of them to confront.

But *the show must go on.* Though there was one show that did not. That happened three months earlier, in August, when John and Jackie's son Patrick died 39 hours after childbirth (not the first or the last of many such Kennedy tragedies). Ed Sullivan cancelled Cliff for the following Sunday and Cliff cancelled himself from that night's performance at the Café Muse.

Given Cliff's superstitious nature, one letter in particular postmarked Dallas, haunted him. Scrawled in lipstick, unsigned, of course, the missive made no overt threat; simply stated facts. Such as the fact that since William B. Harrison, every American president elected in a year ending in zero died while in office.

On a separate page, the letter listed the martyrs: Harrison (1840), Abraham Lincoln (1860), James A. Garfield (1880), William McKinley (1900), Warren G. Harding (1920), Franklin D. Roosevelt (1940).

The last line read as follows: John F. Kennedy, elected 1960.

That one arrived in the mail on Tuesday a week ago intercepted, as usual, by Cliff's uptown agent and manager Paul Hogan, or rather by a woman who was part of Cliff Harris' letter-reading team, hired by Hogan. Hogan was disinclined to share this libel with Cliff as Cliff was getting rattled by the enveloping mean-spiritedness; bitterness was starting to show up in his performances. He'd begun to snap at hecklers.

Ed Sullivan took note of this new more brittle Cliff Harris. Brashness was fine, but sullenness was out. Sullivan now insisted that Cliff's material be approved beforehand. No more ad libs. Cliff asked: "Is America still a nation or have we simply become an audience?" Open to pop but dead to the challenge of ideas, was what he meant.

Today he was doing Paul Hogan a favor. No overcoat. Soon after the flare-up at Smitty's he was prepared to hail a cab when he felt his throat tighten. He began to retch and gag and there at the corner of 63rd and Second Avenue, right outside Adam and Eve's, he leaned over the sidewalk to puke. The waste got on his clothes. Horrified pedestrians gave him a wide circle. Cabs ignored his hand signals.

He walked down as far as 54th and Third and there stopped in for a few more rounds at P.J. Clarke's. Outside again he began to sob silently. He sobbed for himself. He sobbed for everybody, even his father whom he had loved and hated and who had died a drowning death in Africa (while doing *God's Work*), on this very day, November 22, 1952.

There was too much going on and it had all begun to catch up to Cliff. He was afraid to be John Kennedy, he was afraid not to be John Kennedy. He was sick of being loved; he was sick of being hated. He was tired of going up before the people to do tricks.

Soon, after he washed up, changed, and pulled himself together, he'd stand before another crowd greedy for entertainment, another crowd but all the same. They were all the same and they all terrified him. They wanted something from him that he did not have, that even the real Kennedy did not have. They wanted a *Messiah*. They wanted to be young forever and to live forever. They did not care for the *pursuit* of happiness. They wanted happiness period. Meanwhile they'd settle for the dream, and the jokes; the dream from JFK, the jokes from Cliff.

First he'd have to get a cab and in his putrid condition this was not happening, so he began to walk and to reflect, even going over his zingers. He'd jest again about the Peace Corps, plus add another wisecrack in connection with those American students who had defied the law and visited Cuba.

When asked about it at a news conference, JFK smiled and said, "Why shouldn't they go? If I were 21 years old, that's what I would do this summer."

To which Cliff had added: "Well, folks, I'm back!" Suggesting that Kennedy was 21.

That one was sure to work again this afternoon. Nothing could fail if it dealt with John Kennedy's youthfulness. Nor Jackie Kennedy's love of glitter and opulence. Following the death of her newborn son, she had gone off to Greece alone to spend some time to recuperate. There she met shipping tycoon Aristotle Onassis.

There had to be some good lines there, good, but not offensive, for no American audience, even in irreverent Greenwich Village, would tolerate or forgive a slight against Jackie's honor. She was the perfect wife, the most loyal First Lady. She had invented that adoring gaze adopted by every First Lady since.

Not everything, even besides Jackie, was fodder for yucks. There wasn't much humor in the Freedom March on Washington for civil rights, and nothing hilarious about the Atomic Test Ban treaty.

Khrushchev wasn't a laugh a minute, even though he was so easy to lampoon. But there was nothing really humorous about a guy who kept saying he intended to annihilate America, as meanwhile he had his finger on the pulse of 40,000 missiles. There was nothing funny about Castro.

Nor was there much mirth to the Rev. Martin Luther King, Jr., or Malcolm X.; America's increasing involvement in Vietnam was no rib-tickler, either, what with American "advisors" starting to come under attack. The term "body bags" was starting to become familiar.

But the jokes had to keep on coming. Or else he was useless. What's more, oh how the people detested Cliff when for a moment he turned serious. The people felt betrayed. Despite problems here and abroad, America was in a lighthearted mood, in a mood for Barbie dolls and Beatles. With Kennedy at the helm, America was going places, restless as always but finally, after Eisenhower, on the move.

America was getting so big and full of itself that John Kennedy had to promise it the moon!

Or, on the other hand, there was this: The nation was so beset by problems, so concerned over nuclear warfare (chastened by the Cuban missile crisis), so fretful about the division of the races, so alarmed at the stirrings of Black Power, so worried about the growing rift between the rich and the poor, that it insisted on humor as a diversion.

That's where Bob Hope, Jack Benny, Martin and Lewis, Jackie Gleason, George and Gracie Allen, Steve Allen, George Gobel, Joey Adams came in to answer the call for frivolity - not to forget the most important jester of them all at the moment, Cliff Harris.

Jester, court jester, that was a pejorative he labeled upon himself for having the *chutzpah* to do Kennedy. He, Cliff Harris, was not the man who had coined the phrase of the 60's: America would "pay any price, bear any burden, meet any hardship, support any friend, oppose any foe to assure the survival and the success of liberty."

That was John F. Kennedy who said that, not Cliff Harris.

Upon such reflections, Cliff felt himself less of an impersonator and more of an imposter.

In his own estimation he was not big enough to be Kennedy and he barely sized up as Cliff Harris.

At 49th and Third he stopped to catch his breath. He had already covered more than 20 blocks on foot and had begun to stagger. He had been walking like a thief against the sides of the buildings. Nobody recognized him as one of the most famous men in America. He barely thought himself in America. Everything seemed like wilderness. What was this place? Who were these people?

He'd had these attacks before, wherein he felt so lost, a lonely man in a lonely land.

He was in a dark mood when at 48th and Third he finally got a cab to stop for him. He gave the address at the Café Muse. Mistake. Usually he knew better but today he forgot. "That's where that Kennedy guy does his stuff," said the cabbie. Cliff said nothing. "Yeah," said the cabbie, eyeing Cliff from the rearview mirror. "Cliff Harris, right? Biggest show in town. Say, what do you think happens to that guy if Kennedy ever got killed?"

There it was again, but he let it go. But it still gave him the willies. Was there a death wish afoot in the nation, or was his mere presence a provocation? Come on, do not let them get to you Cliff reminded himself as he felt the onset of a new eczema attack, over which the doctors had recommended R&R - and not to take life so hard! So far the splotches arrived only on occasion and had not yet reached his face - for which he thanked God even though he did not believe in God. The god he did believe in was a prankster, a comedian like himself. Look around - wasn't it all a joke?

"Remember when Kennedy himself was in town last week?" the cabbie persisted. "Somebody ran out of the crowd and took a shot at him, I mean with a camera. I was there. Shoulda seen the Secret Service gone nuts. Say..."

Now the cabbie took a good look at Cliff. There wasn't much to recognize. His hair was a mess, his clothes were splattered with vomit - not much of a resemblance even to himself. But New York cabbies were savvy. "Say, is that you?"

"No, it's not me."

Cliff paid the fare and ducked in the back entrance of the Café Muse.

"Holy shit!" said Gloria MacKenzie. "What the fuck happened to you?"

Chapter 8

Bleecker Street was beginning to sizzle. As Cliff showered and dressed and rehearsed his Kennedy gestures in the back room, outside it was mayhem. People were jumping out of moving cars to get a place in line and the line was beginning to stretch all the way up to the Village Gate, where bartender Dick Foy - originally a tree surgeon - began serving drinks to the frost-nipped and the thirsty. Horns blaring, people shouting, waving, laughing. All this tumult with   plenty of time before showtime. This ritual was played out every night, but today it was under the noonday sun.

Gloria MacKenzie, finally recovering from the fright Cliff had given her when he arrived beaten and soaked in puke, stepped outside to take measure of the crowd. She seldom smiled, but she was happy. She was happy except for one thing: There were two uptown cops here to see her from the 17th Precinct. That made no sense. If there had been trouble it would have been downtown, here, not uptown. This was Sixth Precinct territory. The uptown officers gave their names as Sgt. Ron DeVito and Sgt. Frank Toscano and she had them waiting in her office while she checked out the crowd.

That came first, before anything. Box office was life and death. So they'd have to wait as she sized up the crowd. But she was concerned, almost expecting a visit like this from the time, more than a month ago, she read something in the *New York Post* about a man on East 82nd Street, Yorkville, who had died bitten by a cobra. The incident made front page in the *New York Post*, a newspaper everybody read and trusted. The *New York Post* was famed for its hard-hitting news, its Hemingway style of sharp, decisive sentences and for its literate editorials. The name of the victim sounded slightly familiar. Possibly an accident, said the authorities, but the investigation continues. Well, she thought, we'll see.

Outside she noted Texas drawls, Alabama twangs, Indiana crew cuts and clear-eyed self-satisfied faces that could only mean Ohio, Nebraska, Iowa, Missouri, Montana, Wyoming. Lenny Bruce, between prisons and not usually on the street this early in the day were it not for Cliff, ambled by and whispered to Gloria: "How come *you* get all the *goyim?*"

These *goyim* from the heartland were waiting for Cliff to zing them with his new *Fronteah*, his *Cuber* for Cuba, his pay any *priche*, his *bayeah* any burden. The women wore their hair in bouffant, just like Jackie. Some wore pillbox hats just like Jackie.

There were whistles and gasps and finger-pointing from the tourists (all Cleveland, as Richie Bell would say) when they spotted Barbra Streisand driving by. She was then appearing at the Bon Soir up the street but had been introduced to America on Joe Franklin's TV show when she had appeared on a panel with Jack Lalanne and Rudy Vallee.

More ogling when they saw the slouching Bob Dylan emerge with his guitar from the Café Wha, and here came Shelley Berman from out the Bitter End after a meeting with Fred Weintraub - and wasn't that Peter, Paul and Mary across the street, and gosh, Helen, I know Mary, but which one's Peter and which one's Paul?

Gloria assessed this as a good crowd. Unlike some jaded New Yorkers they had come happy and would leave happy.

They were not asking for much. They were asking for a laugh and their own piece of Kennedyana. These were not critical-minded intellectuals.

These were not elitists. These did not subscribe to *Commentary* or *New York Review of Books*. They read *Life* and the *Saturday Evening Post*. These were bedrock, Main Street Americans and America, generally speaking, was in a good mood; almost giddy.

Why not? The *New York Post* said the U.S. economy was thriving. The annual Gross National Product, Huntley and Brinkley reported on NBC, had grown 100 billion dollars since Kennedy's inaugural.

That was the magic word: Kennedy. He set the trend.

On Kennedy's urging, America was in the middle of a physical fitness craze. Bad back and all, he set the example yachting and playing football. He was lean and trim. America saw itself as lean and trim. He was the exemplar of youth and fitness, and what was America if not the newly invigorated first world power! The Soviets had beaten us into space but the preeminence would soon be ours with the Saturn rocket set to be launched next month.

Even the hard-bitten prove-it-to-me New Yorkers were here today with an eager countenance. They too were smitten.

Only last week Kennedy had visited Manhattan and had been swamped. Near the Village - actually near the Café Muse where his double was performing - Kennedy had torn free from his Secret Service detail to mix with the elated multitudes, who gaped upon him as though he were king and movie star rolled into one.

Then, back in the presidential limo, now stuck in traffic, a photographer broke from the crowd and shot the president. That night, Walter Cronkite, who along with millions of other Americans had begun to worry about Kennedy's recklessness in crowds, said of that Instamatic camera - "Good thing it wasn't a gun."

Officers DeVito and Toscano were polite and friendly - but they were *police officers*, and to top it off police officers from the 17th Precinct which Gloria knew covered the east side of Manhattan. Odd numbers were used for the east; even numbers for the west. Gloria knew that, and she also knew that Richie Bell lived on *east* 82nd Street before coming to the Village.

Just an informal inquiry, said the officers. Just checking if she knew about that possible homicide that had made headlines a few weeks back in connection with a man who had died as the result of a snake bite, in his home.

No, she lied, she had not read about it as she seldom read newspapers save the *Village Voice*. The officers smiled at a remark that typified the Village. That's right, people here are too busy reading poetry.

We do not watch television either, Gloria added for good measure, and listen to radio only sometimes. Informal inquiry my eye, she thought. I am in for a grilling. What she had suspected and feared may be true after all.

Well, said the police officers, we do not wish to take up too much of your time, we know you have a show to put on but...does the name Timothy B. Baines mean anything to you? No, she said, the name means nothing to me.

Then how about the name Richie Bell?

Gloria gulped and sat frozen in her seat, and the police officers, being police officers with a nose for deception, were alert to her stupification. They watched her closely as she recovered, and then snapped that of course she knew Richie Bell. Richie Bell was working as a waiter at the Village Gate, was staying beyond the summer - away from Hartford and Harvard - for the fun and the excitement and the chance to make it as a folksinger.

"Is he a friend of yours?"

"He's my lover."

Though astonished by such an unexpected burst of candor, the officers played deaf for the most part. Again, Greenwich Village, and that's how people here talked and that's what people here did.

Was she aware of a connection between Richie Bell and the deceased Mr. Baines?

She held her tongue as the officers now pulled their chairs closer in anticipation.

But her reply would take some time. This was serious business and each word would count. Perhaps it was already time for a lawyer but that in itself would raise suspicion and take this beyond the bounds of an "informal inquiry." So maybe she ought to take the tough broad approach. After all, she was a tough broad. Everyone in the Village thought so.

One cross look from those bloodshot eyes and people knew to take a hike. But cops weren't people. Cops were cops. These cops, civil as they were, would not be so easy to brush off.

Now of course she knew of a connection between Richie Bell and Tim Baines. For a while Richie talked about nothing else - and then dropped the subject as though something had happened. They had arrived in New York together from Hartford, found as apartment on East 82nd, and Tim, ugly and obnoxious, found a job immediately as a corporate photographer. Handsome Richie could not find work and was broke. Yes he could always count on Dad back home in Hartford but the entire reason for coming to New York was to make it on your own.

So Richie kept on being broke and Tim kept on paying the rent on the provision that he'd be reimbursed once

Richie got on his feet - maybe in Greenwich Village, where Richie kept auditioning but to no avail.

Bitterness began to set in on Tim's part when, back on 82nd Street, Richie had all the girls. Tim could not even get the leftovers. Tim was short and to make himself taller he ordered Richie to do the dishes, mop the floors and clean out the toilet since these chores fell to Richie as the free-loader between the two.

Tim liked to shout these orders just when Richie was romancing some girl. He timed it just right.

"Later, man."

"Now! Man!"

Richie being Richie, a golden boy who took everything in stride, shrugged off these affronts with his customary smile, but inwardly he began to smolder. Finally he landed that job in the Village at the Village Gate and began paying off the monetary debt to Tim paycheck by paycheck.

Tim, now living alone on 82nd Street as Richie had moved on to Sullivan Street in the Village, showed up promptly at 11 p.m. every Friday to collect. Tim's very presence infuriated Richie. Tim did not belong. He was not downtown. He walked around in a suit and tie and crew cut and kept asking where the orgies were. Tim wasn't even uptown, and not even Hartford. As he continued to pay off Tim Friday by Friday, Richie wondered how he had ever allowed Tim to become a friend, which of course he wasn't anymore. He was a bill collector.

Finally, the bill was paid off, by Richie's reckoning. But not by Tim's. Tim continued to show up at the Village Gate demanding more money and insisting that Richie include him as "part of the gang." He wanted orgies, and more money. Tim was becoming more than a pest and a nuisance. He was an embarrassment. Just by showing up in the Village he was defiling the place. He was a bloodsucker. The torment had to end.

"Yes," Gloria finally conceded. "There was a connection between Richie Bell and Tim Baines."

"They had shared an apartment on 82ⁿᵈ Street, right?"

"I think so."

"Now," said Officer DeVito, "which one of them had a snake as a pet?"

Gloria lit up her tenth cigarette and coughed. She'd been coughing throughout from a lifetime of smokes.

"Snake?"

"One of them had a pet snake, the same snake that did in Mr. Baines."

"What kind of a snake?" said Gloria, stalling for time.

"Northern Copperhead. Very deadly," said Officer Toscano.

"Can't help you there," said Gloria.

"You don't know if Richie Bell kept a snake," said Officer DeVito.

"No, and even if the snake did belong to Richie, it could all have been an accident."

"That's what we're trying to figure out," said Officer Toscano.

"Could easily have been an accident, but it's important for us to find out whose pet it was," said Officer DeVito.

"Look," said Gloria, calling on her tough side, "whatever happened uptown happened uptown. This is the Village."

Both officers folded their note books, got up and thanked her for her time. They complimented her on the success of her club and promised to catch the show someday. Gloria said any time.

When they left, Gloria helped herself to three straight shots of Johnny Walker. Then she broke into tears.

Chapter 9

Cliff had his make-up on and even so concluded there was still time. He'd taken a peek outside, saw the commotion, and decided that he really wasn't ready for these people just yet and that if the show started late it would not be the end of the world. He needed more lubrication and he needed company. Unlike Gloria, and perhaps the rest of the Village, he did watch television. He had to, to keep up with Kennedy - keep the image alive and before his eyes. He needed to constantly observe his man for inspiration. He had to keep up with the news as the latest Kennedy remark might be useful as material - that way his material stayed fresh and timely.

Right now, on CBS, Kennedy was in a Dallas motorcade with Jackie. The announcer said the president was in Dallas to support a candidate whose name Cliff did not catch. All he saw was Jack smiling and waving to the crowds. Even though the TV was black and white and the images of the president somewhat blurred in this fleeting news report, Cliff noticed something that most people miss. Kennedy looked tired, and a bit old, despite the show of vivacity.

No question about it, the man had aged, and may even be suffering. He had a bad back, but in nearly three years in the White House he'd also had his share of setbacks and it was beginning to show. This was something Cliff had to take into consideration. The time might come when he'd have to revise his act and display a more seasoned Kennedy. He had to be ready. In fact, he was more than ready.

Now he needed a drink and the company of good friends and the place for that was McSorley's Old Ale House on the east side. He ducked out the back entrance of the Café Muse and hailed a cab on Bleecker and MacDougal and got in   before he could be mobbed. Even so a few tourists caught sight of him and took chase, though to no avail. Cliff caught a glimpse of his pursuers and shook his head. He could not understand the need people had to touch their icons. Indeed, there were no icons, only ordinary men and women with a gift for this or that - sometimes no gift other than good looks, like Tab Hunter - but people lifted up these ordinary men and women and made them gods; worshiped them   upon the high places and demanded autographs.

Why, Cliff wondered today and always - why this need for autographs? Why this obsession with celebrity? Ben had once told him that it was a genetic reflex that dated back to the days of idol worship. Made sense. People needed gods, even if they were false gods.

The McSorley Roundtable was in session. (With the notable absence of Richie Bell, licking his wounds inflicted by Louise Carmen.) Cliff smiled warmly. His spirits were lifted at the comforting sight of Lenny Bruce sitting here with Joe Franklin, Ben Jaffa, Louise Carmen, and just in from Atlantic City was his pal Sonny Schwartz.

Dressed as a stereotypical hippie, which almost hid his movie-star chiseled features, Sonny was doing journalistic undercover for the *Atlantic City Gazette* to infiltrate the Sundeens who were threatening to blow up buildings in New York and Atlantic City. (Later in the 60's, they would succeed in blowing up a Greenwich Village building in which Dustin Hoffman had an apartment. Actually, this occurred in 1968 when everything was being blown up.)

Sonny's life was constantly at risk from this undercover work and not even his friends, plus his beloved girlfriend Connie, whom he would shortly marry, knew about his double-life, though she suspected. (The authorities, acting on his inside information, had already credited him with preventing three major catastrophes that were in the pipe-line by the Sundeens and related groups.) To the public, however, Sonny was known as a popular Atlantic City radio host who had, in fact, given Cliff Harris his very first shot on the air. The tape of that classic show got Cliff to Joe Franklin, from there it was on to Ed Sullivan...

Sonny, an honorary member of the Sullivan Street Irregulars, opened with:

"We were just leaving to see *you* pal! What's up?"

"Needed a break," said Cliff patting backs all around and offering Louise Carmen a big fat kiss.

"That's more than Ben's been getting," mumbled Lenny, to which Louise responded by pouring pepper into his scotch.

"A break? From what?" said Ben, feigning irritation as Cliff seated himself amid the warmth of the group, his hands shaking until he downed the first of several vodkas.

But he was in high spirits, especially animated by the news he was about to reveal.

"From all the shit. You see what's going on out there? Nothing but people."

"Isn't that the general idea?" said Joe, laughing. "Since when is standing-room only a complaint?"

"He resents you guys," Ben cracked, speaking to Sonny and Joe. "You made him rich and famous. You bastards."

"He wants obscurity," said Sonny, nodding at Cliff as to a misunderstood kid brother.

"Come on," said Louise Carmen, her cheeks aflame from the bonhomie and smiling gently at Cliff. "He wants peace."

"You get that when you're dead," snapped Lenny without intending to be cruel or funny and in fact, here in private, among his peers and his cronies, Lenny Bruce was anything but the brash and vulgar satirist that he was on stage. He was almost shy, and nearly a conformist, dressed in a black suit, conservative tie, hair cropped short and neat. He could pass for a rabbi or perhaps a seminary student and even in his quick-moving piercing dark eyes and restless herky-jerky countenance he could be taken for a scholar keen to return to his studies at the Yeshiva.

"Seriously," said Joe. "Isn't your show soon to go on?"

To Joe Franklin, show business was serious business. Despite being of the same generation, he acted the part of father to the group. By his radio and TV shows on WOR he had helped make and shape dozens of careers but in his world there were no stars. It was plain hard work that got you to the top, and it was even harder work to stay on top.

"I've got something big to tell you *shumcks*," said Cliff, playing with a sly grin.

"You're gonna donate your teeth to the Smithsonian," said Lenny.

"When you stop wearing brown shoes," said Cliff.

"What's this with you and teeth?" Joe wanted to know from Lenny.

"Do me something, I'm big on teeth. *Goyim* have all the teeth. We have the noses. Look at you Cliff!"

"Hereditary. Like your frown."

"Now Louise, babe," Lenny said. "You've got the greatest teeth, and they're not even *goyim* teeth."

"That's my Jewish soul."

"From a truck stop like Wheeling, West Virginia?"

"I never said I was Jewish. But I must have a Jewish soul. There's a rumor my great-grandfather had some Jewish blood."

"Everybody's grandfather had some Jewish blood."

"Everybody's grandfather is Jewish," said Ben.

"Everybody old is Jewish," said Sonny. "All Jewish people are old, all old people are Jewish."

"So what's the hot news, Cliff?" said Joe.

"There's a change in the wind."

"Oh no," Ben groaned. Ben the doorman but really the wisdom-giver of the group. "Not again, Cliff. Please!"

"This time I'm doing it," announced Cliff with fanfare.

"Doing what?" asked Lenny, curious as only a fellow entertainer would be. Lenny, ace social commentator and iconoclast that he was, might be counted among those who considered Cliff a sellout since Cliff's humor was conventional, not biting satire like his own. But he kept an open mind about Cliff and did admire the man's skill, as Kennedy. Anyway, and most important, he liked Cliff.

"You know that hotline that just got hooked up between Washington and Moscow?" Cliff began, already checking around the table for assent. "Okay? The one between Jack and Nikita just in case somebody makes a mistake and presses the wrong button? Now suppose Nikita *does* press the wrong button and there's missiles coming our way. Jack gets on the hotline phone..."

"I see where this is going," said Lenny, eyes narrowing in reproach. "We start trading cities."

"That's right," said Cliff. "You polished off New York, Nikita, so we get Moscow. Detroit for Leningrad. Philadelphia for Stalingrad. Just to keep it fair, and here's the kicker, man, they're going about it matter-of-factly. Like it's regular business. They're actually doing it to save the rest of the world, so they've agreed to go at it tit for tat, and Kennedy chooses specific targets - those cities that have mostly blacks and gays and other people considered so undesirable."

"Sounds too sick for me," said Lenny, unsmiling and shaking his head.

"This from the king of sick?"

"No," said Ben. "What Lenny means is that it's just plain sick. Period."

"It's not comedy," added Sonny.

Like Joe Franklin, Sonny Schwartz was a champion to the stars. It was his view that entertainers were more than court jesters. They were public figures upon whom the public had invested its trust. Loyalty and integrity were expected and demanded in return. To switch character midstream, as Cliff was suggesting, would be an abomination. Moreover, in Sonny's other life as an undercover investigative reporter, he was seeing enough of *sick*.

"Maybe I don't want to do comedy. Milton Berle does *comedy*."

"Cliff wants to do philosophy," Ben offered.

"Stand-up philosophy," snapped Sonny.

"Shmigegee here wants to kill the goose that laid the Kennedy egg," said Lenny.

"When do you plan to do this?" asked Joe, alarmed.

"Why not this afternoon?" said Cliff.

"Good a time as any to commit suicide," said Ben.

"As John Kennedy?" said Joe, getting more upset by the minute.

"Yup."

"Cliff," said Louise, taking a motherly approach. "That's so out of character. I mean Jack Kennedy being so cynical?"

"The good guy in all of us is just a front, a façade," said Cliff, making his point as to a class that needed heavy persuasion. "That's what I plan to show. We're all phony and evil. We all have a dark side."

"Not all of us," said Louise emphatically. "Sorry, but you've got it all wrong, Cliff."

"Heavy stuff," said Joe, clearly perturbed. "Cliff, this can ruin your career. Ben's not kidding about suicide."

"I already hear the toilet flushing," said Lenny.

"Maybe even ruin Kennedy himself," said Sonny. "I mean you two are in this thing together. Like it or not."

"He doesn't like it," said Ben.

"That's right I don't," said Cliff.

"We're not talking some skit here, Cliff," Joe said. "We're not even talking career. We're talking your life. The image. You can't just go out there and spit on the people. Can't do it Cliff. Think this over very carefully. Be deliberate in judgment, as the saying goes."

"Better yet," said Louise. "Don't judge!"

"Really," said Joe. "Think it over."

"I did. I've been thinking it over for months, and it's time."

"What exactly is it you're trying to say in this shtick?" Sonny asked. "I mean besides the fact that you're nuts."

"I just told you. I'm showing that human nature is basically bad. We're all evil at the core."

"When did you arrive at that conclusion?" asked Ben.

"Every day. Beginning with my dad. Long story."

"So let's ask the Biblical expert," said Sonny. "Ben? What's the Jewish take on this?"

"People are basically good," Louise jumped in.

"To you," said Lenny, "because you're beautiful."

"She has good teeth," said Sonny.

"That's so unfair," said Louise with conviction followed by the trace of a smile.

"I know," said Lenny, nodding in that deep-in-thought style of his, finger to lips, head bowed in contemplation, to emerge, as on stage, with his morsel of profundity. "Life's unfair except to the rich and beautiful."

"Life's not so fair to them, either," countered Louise. "Don't be so sure."

"But it does help," said Ben, straight-faced but enjoying it all.

"But Ben!" said Louise. "You've got everything. You're handsome..."

"I'm halfway there," said Ben. "Next stop is rich."

"You've got me, darling," Louise said delightedly and striking a pose.

"Halfway there, too."

"Ben, Ben, Ben," she chuckled.

"So," Sonny persisted, "what does the Jewish religion say about out being basically good or evil? To you, Ben."

But Louise had the answer. "The Bible says, we're all basically good," she said proudly.

"Wrong," said Ben. "The Bible says we're all rotten. That's why there is a Bible, man, to keep us from doing all that shit we did before we had rules. Human sacrifice, child sacrifice, incest, random murder, rape..."

"So what's changed?" asked Cliff.

"Just another day in the big city anyway," said Lenny.

"So imagine a world without the Ten Commandments," said Ben. "We'd be living in Sodom."

"I kinda like Sodom," said Lenny.

"You would," said Louise. "That's where the word sodomize comes from."

"I love it when you talk dirty," said Sonny.

"She hasn't even started," said Ben.

"Oh, fuck, Ben, I don't talk dirty."

"My grandfather came from Sodom," said Lenny. "He was a rag merchant. Sold *shmattehs*."

"Same stuff you're still selling," said Cliff.

"Retail, not wholesale like you," said Lenny.

"How come you still get your hair cut in Brooklyn?" Joe asked Cliff.

"I got a guy there gives me the best razor job."

"Never mind the manicurist who gives the best blow job," said Ben.

"So that's what they mean by blow dry," said Louise.

"There's Frank's right here on Horatio does just as good a job."

"Blow jobs?" said Cliff.

"Razor cuts," said Joe.

"Guess I'm still waiting on the Dodgers," said Cliff. "Talk about the dark side of human nature."

"Enough with the dark side," said Lenny. "I thought we settled the matter. What we're saying is fuck you, Cliff, and fuck that shit routine you're trying to sell. Keep the franchise. Jesus Christ."

"You just used the Lord's name in vain," said Sonny.

"I'm allowed. He's family."

At the urging and inspiration of Ben Jaffa, Lenny Bruce was working on just such a routine, based on the premise - He may be God to you, *to us He's family*. We did not reject Him. We just don't accept the guy playing stickball with us as a God! Like this: A Jewish family in Jerusalem is sitting around the dinner table when the daughter arrives home star struck saying, *I just heard the most incredible sermon!*

Where? says the skeptical mother.

On the Mount.

A sermon on the Mount? So who gave this sermon on the Mount?

Jesus.

So who is Jesus?

"God."

Are we talking about the same Jesus? The kid with the runny nose from Nazareth? Jake the carpenter's boy? This is God? Oy gevalt!

"Ben," said Cliff, still seeking approval for his new shtick. "You do agree man is basically evil."

"As a matter of life? Yes. As comedy? No."

"But you do agree that we're all made up of two parts, one good, one bad. Come on, Ben, you were there!"

"Look," said Ben, holding up his arms in surrender. "Yes, we all have that other side and you never know what can provoke it, okay? There I'm with you, Cliff. Sometimes it's merely a guy cutting in front of you, and sometimes it's a leader who's brainwashed the people. Me, for example - I mean I hate to be at a party where people are drunk. A couple of whiskies and Mr. Nice Guy turns into a racist and a bigot and he even looks and sounds different. My question always is, are the drinks revealing him for what he really is? All I'm saying, Cliff - all we're saying - is leave it the fuck alone. This is dangerous territory. People do not come to you for truth. So drop it, Cliff. They come to you for fucking entertainment! Remember?"

"I agree," said Joe. "I urge you to reconsider. Really, the people will not accept an evil John Kennedy."

"It's not Kennedy I'm reflecting here: it's the people."

"But you're Kennedy," said Sonny. "We made you Kennedy. Joe and I helped make you Kennedy."

"You're saying I owe you?"

"I'm saying you owe it to the illusion," said Sonny.

"Fuck illusion. People want truth."

"You know the truth?" said Lenny, eyeing Cliff slowly.

"As much as you do," said Cliff, "and look how much you get away with - when you're not in the Tombs."

"That's because I'm out there on my own. I'm sticking my own neck out. You're sticking out Kennedy's."

"Drop it," said Joe. "Really Cliff, we all worked too hard to get you to where you are today."

"Go on being a hypocrite, right?"

"I really resent that," said Louise, dropping her 19-year-old youthfulness for a moment to sound like the unrevealed sage she really was. "I mean just because we have our bad moments doesn't mean we're hypocrites or that we're bad. If you'd just look for it, you'd find loving kindness in every person."

"Cliff stopped looking a long time ago," shrugged Ben.

"Ben," said Cliff, incredulously, "if anybody should know about the ugly side of human nature, it's you."

"So who better to forget it than me?"

"You're not after the truth?" asked Cliff.

"That's the last thing I'm after."

"Well, that's where we differ, Ben."

"You're in the wrong country if it's truth you're after," said Lenny, showing signs of indignation. "People came to this country to escape the fucking truth. They continue to come for the same reason. Truth is shit. Yeah, Ben knows."

"So what is truth according to Rabbi Lenny Bruce?" said Louise.

"Truth," said Lenny, "is misery and oppression. Truth is sickness of spirit. Truth is all that shit that's happened in Europe over the centuries, up until twenty years ago. Europe was built on the stones of misery. America was built on the foundation of illusion. Truth is Richard Wagner and the old world. Illusion is America and Elvis and I say thank God for illusion."

"A strange commentary coming from Lenny Bruce," said Cliff. "The man out to destroy the system."

"Make that *change* the system," said Lenny. "Anyway I know what's bad, but I likewise know what's worse."

"Can you be more specific?" Louise asked Lenny.

"I thought I was," said Lenny.

"Sonny?" Louise persisted. "What's your take on truth and illusion?"

Louise hungered for knowledge and was not ashamed to ask questions. Her own heroes at the moment were Socrates, Plato, and Aristotle - who along with the Talmudists had pretty much invented the give-and-take. She was starting to read Kierkegaard as existentialism was now making the rounds. Her dream was to settle into old age as an intellectual, preferably a French intellectual, as they, the French, seemed to be doing it with such style and passion. She'd taken a course on Sartre at City College and was even now smoking Gaulois.

"What do I know," said Sonny, yawning from a week of sleepless nights.

"You know plenty," urged Louise. "Stop pretending."

"All right. Illusion means that we expect happiness as our God-given lifetime guarantee," said Sonny. "Truth - the part we're trying to hide - is the fact that life is misery. That's the truth, and like Lenny said, it sucks."

"You don't know what the fuck I'm talking about," said Cliff, somewhat belligerently.

Which was the wrong approach to take with Sonny, who knew all about the indelicate side of human nature from his undercover work. "Listen, man," he said, making no bones about his annoyance. "You think I don't know the dark side? But the dark side is not what you're being paid for, Cliff. That's something *I'm* being paid for, and listen, I'd be happy to trade places with you any day. Never mind the details. You, and yeah, Milton Berle, you guys are our escape hatch. The illusion is what keeps you going, and guess what, it's what keeps us all going. Illusion, man, that's the only thing that separates us from insanity.

"So why not keep the illusion?" said Joe as a peacemaker. "We're doing all right deluding ourselves. Let it be."

"Well thanks for your support," Cliff said getting up and ready to leave in a huff.

"Don't take it the wrong way," said Ben. "On second thought, maybe you should."

That drew cackles, even from Cliff.

"Ben!" Louise protested. "Cliff's your friend!"

"That's what this is all about."

"Cliff's only trying to do something original," Louise said with a straight face. "It sucks, but it's original."

"Oh, thanks, Louise," said Cliff.

"How come you're not on Centre Street this morning?" Sonny asked Lenny.

The Criminal Court House was located at 100 Centre Street, the prison known as the Tombs was right in back on Baxter Street, and if anybody knew about courts and prisons it was Lenny Bruce.

"Sometimes they forget," said Lenny.

"I'll bet that does hurt your feelings," said Ben.

"Sometimes they need to arrest a serial rapist, so they forget about me. Yeah, but it does hurt my feelings."

"I'm outta here," said Cliff. "You guys have been a big help."

"That's why we're here," said Ben. "It's us or Bellevue."

"Have we talked some sense into you?" asked Joe.

"Sense from you characters?"

"Break a leg," Louise called out as Cliff made for the door.

Cliff froze and shook his head and frowned before stepping out.

"That's bad luck," Joe whispered to Louise.

That was the latest taboo. Louise hadn't heard.

Chapter 10

John Kennedy kept calling for sacrifice and this was a summons Ben Jaffa took very seriously. When asked mockingly by his nonconformist friends if he was a patriot, Ben said No, not a patriot, but grateful. He was grateful to be an American. To be an American, by his reckoning, was a gift if not a downright miracle, considering the rest of the world, especially the world of jackboots that he had escaped from as a child. The rest of the world was hell, and yes, America was paradise - not perfect - but paradise by comparison. This passion for his adopted country provoked puzzlement to the point of hostility among his radical friends to whom American citizenship was a birthright and therefore, as Ben saw it, nothing to celebrate. They snubbed a privilege that was sacred to Ben.

Imagine the world, he'd argue, without America. Tell me, where would you go to escape repression and find liberty and the pursuit of happiness and one hour dry cleaning?

For all that and more he had a duty to enlist. The Army, the Navy and Air Force, the Marines - all had turned him down on account of his trick knee, the left knee that had been damaged from a martial arts incident and that had gone on to require three operations.

By persistence, Ben had however developed something of a friendship with a Navy recruitment officer posted at Times Square, Seaman Margus Johnston. Perhaps with some stroking and cunning the man might be persuaded. Ben was determined to serve. Weeks earlier Johnston had sent some papers through and had suggested that there might be a response for Ben later in the month - and this was later in the month. So why not give it a shot? This day was as good as any and so Johnston was Ben's destination, with Louise along for company, and what if they were late for Cliff's matinee? If they were late, so be it, except that Louise was anxious to be there on time just to be sure that they had succeeded in keeping Cliff from going ahead with his dangerous new skit.

Ben Jaffa and Louise Carmen left McSorley's as a couple. Louise, invigorated as always by the McSorley's roundtable debates, was hot to trot. "Let's do something," she said spiritedly as she snuggled up against Ben.

Ben knew the code. Let's go to bed was what she meant, except that it wasn't always bed where they made love. She liked it everywhere but bed, in fact.

For the delicious scandal and danger of it all she provoked him for sex "any time, any place," as he put it, which meant the back rooms of the Bitter End (as Peter, Paul and Mary sang "If I Had A Hammer"), the Bon Soir, the Au Go Go (as Lenny Bruce was *shpritzing* away), the Village Gate (even as Richie was waiting on tables there), the Village Vanguard, the Café Muse (even as Cliff was regaling them with his Kennedy), Jack Delaney's, the Purple Onion, the Duplex, the White Horse Tavern, Jimmy Kelly's, once even in a dressing room at S. Klein's department store on Union Square, and later, still on 14th Street, in the ladies' room at the Academy of Music, another time in the bushes of Washington Square Park to the beat of the bongo drums. In all those places, and more, she unzipped him and barely muffled her cries of delight as she went from orgasm to orgasm.

Why not Macy's window? he asked.

Never Macy's she said in mock reproach. Gimbel's - now flashing him mischievous brown eyes. Why not?

More, more, and more. That was Louise. She was a cupful that runneth over. Ben could hardly keep pace. Her great charm, as Ben saw it, was the love she had of herself. She'd been pampered and spoiled and expected nothing less than every reward life had to offer. She wanted all the sex she could get, but she was similarly wanton about learning. She wanted to experience *everything*.

"Where are we going?" she said as Ben hustled her into a cab.

"It's a surprise."

She dropped her original plan to do some Fifth Avenue shopping. She loved surprises and was radiant at the thought that a new adventure was in the offing. Surprise me, she liked to say most nights after Ben was done his door-man duties at the Bitter End and she had just come off her latest Village Gate performance with the Highlight Singers. Surprise me, she'd say breathlessly, eyes sparkling, pageboy bouncing, her complexion a flared up red from the thrill of being young and alive.

That was one reason she required two lovers at the same time - soon to be three. She needed surprises and no one man had a deep enough reservoir. As soon as one lover tapped out, it was on to the next.

"Why uptown?" she said as they were snuggled in the back seat of the cab, Louise beginning to run her tongue along her lips as she smoothed Ben along the crotch and hinted at something wicked with her prankish eyes. They'd never done it in a cab.

At this moment, so solemn for Ben with the Navy on his mind, he wondered if this young lady ever felt sadness. Yes, he thought, sadness, sorrow, melancholy, regret, remorse. In all the months he had known her he had never caught her downcast. Could she possibly be so cheerful in her inner-most heart? He did not really want to find out. He had yet to meet a woman without a story. They all started off cheerful and then came the stories. Drunken mother, abusive father...and what was Louise's story? We are all hiding something. What was she hiding? Ben wanted to know this and then again he didn't. No, he did not want to find out and learn, for example, that where she came from practically everybody died young.

All over the mining community they died young from lung disease and Louise's family in particular had a history of early death related and unrelated to lung disease. For that reason Louise's mother spoiled her and pampered her and rushed her out of town. Her two brothers had died at the ages of 11 and 13. Practically all her surviving cousins, aunts and uncles were sick or sickly, coughing blood and losing teeth by the fistful.

Louise had seen it all. She'd been entered in all the beauty contests and was forced into daily ballet as a hedge built to shield her from the rot and decay all around. But she had seen it and from seeing it she attained wisdom. Fear as well. Was it her destiny to fail in the outside world only to be sent back teetering to so much squalor? If this was the fate that awaited her - and she feared it was - then there was not a moment to lose in extorting every ounce of her youth. Not a minute to lose before her prophecy came true that in the end it would be Roger poetry by night, the mines by day and a houseful of brats in the Osborne Trailer Park as she aged wrung-out, weary and toothless.

If that was how it was fated to end, she'd have her say first as to the beginning. Thus she began her makeover by changing her name from the ordinary Louise Carmine to the glitzy Carmen.

All that was something Ben was not meant to know. That went for Richie and all the rest as well. She had designed herself to sparkle as an ornament and there'd be no sullenness to erode the finish. She had an image to protect; to be known as wisdom-seeking but untarnished.

In the cab, upon her urging, Ben placed his hand between her legs and searched until he found the toy, as she called it, and working gently, rhythmically he got her to gasp in whimpering spurts from a restrained orgasm. She gladly returned the favor.

"You're a naughty girl," he whispered.

"Only with you."

Only with Richie, too, he thought, but let it pass. Why do damage? He knew how she changed, or the mood changed, when he turned serious, or even merely reflective. There wasn't enough time for that stuff. Life was moving too fast. She wanted him for his depth, yes, but only about general things. Nothing too personal. Nothing too deep where it might hit an exposed nerve. (He hated to be called deep, just as she - like most perky girls - hated to be called perky.)

"Oooh," she laughed gazing down. "I got lipstick on you."

"Of all the wrong places."

"Do you mind?"

"Very much."

"Are we bad?"

"Yes."

"I like being bad. Isn't it fun? Being good is so boring. What else can we do?"

"Isn't this enough?"

"For now. I'll think of something," she said determinedly.

"You always do."

"I do like sex," she said.

"Stop the presses."

"But there's got to be something else."

"What kind of kicks are you after, Louise?"

"Anything," she declared.

* * *

They got off several blocks short of Times Square just to do some uptown prancing. They were down in the Village so much that Ben forgot all about men wearing suits and women wearing dresses *and* suits. Ben felt a bit dizzy from the frenzy of business and shopping and he felt very much out of place in his long hair and tall boots. He was aware of being noticed as beat and Bohemian. He seldom thought of himself in those terms.

But compared to the elegance of uptown men and women he was a hippie all right and it was these people, these rush, rush, rush, hardboiled squares talking business and industry that had the world by the balls. They owned the world; the Village was merely renting.

Greenwich Village wasn't real life; merely a diversion to these people. At night they came for the wails of protest from Joan Baez and Judy Collins and for the songs of love, brotherhood and freedom from Peter, Paul and Mary - the words of "Kumbayah," "Michael Row Your Boat," "If I Had A Hammer," "This Land Is Your Land," and "Puff the Magic Dragon" drawing some puzzlement but meeting with approval.

They came to hear Lenny Bruce rip the Establishment. They laughed at their own hypocrisies. They roared as Lenny and Mort Sahl and Richard Pryor poked fun at them, them and their phony liberalism, Lenny saying: Dig, you truly believe in integration? You'll fight for it to the death? Okay, here's your choice. You can marry a white, white woman, or a black, black woman. The white, white woman is Kate Smith. The black, black woman is Lena Horne. Now make your choice.

So hip! They even snapped their fingers as all good weekend hippies were taught to do.

But then they returned to their Wall Streets, their Madison Avenues, their Seventh Avenues to continue the commerce that made the nation go round. Nothing really changed. At night they put on their jeans and their sandals and came so ready to take part in the hipness that was sweeping the land.

They sat on the sawdust floors, sipped the cider handed to them by svelte ebony waiters, cracked open the peanut shells and snapped their fingers in approval to Bob Dylan's "Blowin' in the Wind."

Uptown was foreign. But actually it was the Village that was foreign. Ben just figured that out.

"I wonder where we are going," she said, squeezing Ben's hand in anticipation.

"I want you to be a witness to something."

He wanted her to be there in case there was good news from Johnston. He wanted her to share his pride.

"Can't wait."

"Neither can I."

"Ben," she said, stopping him for a moment's reflection. "There's something I have to tell you."

She told him about Wheeling and Roger and how badly Richie was taking it all.

"You don't mind, do you?"

"Of course I mind," he said, but without much conviction. Yes he did mind but hadn't Richie nailed it when he said, Ben, you act like you're just visiting? Precisely so, thought Ben, even as he was mildly astonished at Louise's revelation and her casual approach to an upcoming round of sex with an old boyfriend. But as a *visitor*, a man going through life without roots, someone just passing through with no notion of loyalty, the most he could ask of Louise was her liveliness and her divided adoration of him.

"You don't sound terribly jealous. Not like Richie. Richie went bananas. He killed his guitar when I told him," she said unable to contain her delight at the effect she had on at least one of her lovers.

"Well I don't have a guitar."

"Stop being cute."

"You've got your mind made up, right?" he said dismissively, though in fact he was indeed slightly pained. If he did not love her with Richie's passion and abandon, he knew one thing: there would never be another Louise.

"I don't. But Roger does." She went into the story of how "persuasive" Roger could be.

Besides, she owed him.

"You owe him?"

"He's an old boyfriend."

"You owe him?"

"Stop it, Ben."

"You owe him?"

"Ben, stop it."

"Tell me I'm not hearing this."

"You're silly."

"Do you love him - this Roger?"

"No."

"But you owe him?"

"Yes."

Ben took a deep breath of submissive incredulity. "I mean isn't sex supposed to be related to love or something?"

"You don't understand."

"I once thought I did."

"You're *impossible*."

Ben shrugged. "It's your life."

"You really don't care. Don't you love me?" she asked desperately.

"Of course I love you."

"Just a little bit?"

"Just a little bit."

"Will you welcome me back?"

"Always."

"You don't love me as much as Richie does," she said petulantly.

Louise could pout with the best of them. Ben could never be sure when her peevishness was sincere or merely another Louise Carmen performance. She knew all the tricks, that was for sure. That was for damned sure and she even had some new ones all her own.

The subject of Richie and three-in-love seldom came up openly between Ben and Richie. The exception came when they both went shopping along Houston for a pair of boots similar to the kind Richard Burton wore that time he and Liz came to the Village for Cliff Harris, and out of the limo stepped Burton with that Churchillian flair and those magnificent boots.

As they walked and talked Richie turned solemn - solemn for Richie - and out of nowhere Richie asked Ben how serious Ben was about Louise. Ben said he liked her very much. Okay, he loved her. But was he prepared to marry her? No, said Ben. In that case, said Richie, you must tell her, otherwise you're guilty of deception and stringing the poor girl along.

That was an accusation and Ben was offended. I thought we were all just having fun, said Ben, though I know, he added, that to girls there's fun and there's romance and love. Exactly, said Richie. So do you love her enough to marry her?

Again Ben said, I love her, but I do not intend to marry her. I love everything about her, but I do not love her as a wife.

Then Ben put the same question to Richie. At the drop of a hat, that's how quickly I'd marry her, said Richie.

So you're saying I should get out of the way and leave you two alone?

Richie did not respond, but to Ben the answer was clear: He was trespassing upon another man's territory. This was more than about love and romance, it was about the territorial imperative.

So Ben, provoked into fairness, tried to distance himself from Louise. That was some weeks back and Louise had been unaware of the reason behind Ben's sudden frigidness.

All it took was one come-hither glance to bring Ben back to the fold and the subject never came up again between Richie and Ben and they never got around to finding those boots either.

* * *

UNCLE SAM WANTS YOU!

"We're going in here?" said Louise in alarm.

"Just for a minute."

She began pulling him away as he made for the door of the recruitment center.

"This is the surprise?" she said.

"It's something I have to do," Ben said firmly.

"No you don't, Ben!" Her eyes were beginning to brim with tears. Ben was astonished at the power of her reaction.

"Yes I do, Louise."

"You're insane. Ben, this isn't for you!"

"Why not?"

"It's for people who kill and get killed."

"I'm not getting killed."

"So what's it all about?"

"It's about, well, it's about serving your country."

"Oh, Ben! Not that horseshit. Not you."

"Yes, me."

"I never thought you took it seriously. You, a soldier?"

"Me, a soldier."

"Soldiers die, Ben."

"I'm not dying so fast."

"They're going to ship you out!"

"To where? Norfolk?" Ben quipped.

"To Vietnam."

"That's only for advisors. How do you know about Vietnam?"

"I see. I'm just some silly little girl who doesn't know about these things."

"There's no Vietnam. There's nothing. It's just me and a uniform - if they take me. I thought you'd be proud."

"Proud of what? You coming back in a box?"

"Now you *are* being a silly little girl."

"Don't go in, Ben. Please!"

For a moment Louise thought she detected the real reason.

"I won't go with Roger," she said.

Ben laughed, and then he hugged her as a father hugs a daughter.

"It's not about Roger," he said holding her as she trembled in his arms.

"Then I don't know what it's about," she whimpered.

She never would know what it's about, except that it was something that men did. Really, it was something that boys did to become men and Louise would never understand the need of it, or the glory of it, or the sense of it, or even the compulsion to prove something. Prove what, and to whom? She needed no proving. Things were fine as they were. She did not need to be persuaded that Ben was a hero. In her eyes, he already was. There were those stories about him but even without those stories he was gallant and dashing.

"One last time," she said. "Don't go."

But Ben went. She waited outside and it had been years since she prayed and now she prayed.

So did Ben, and when he emerged she could tell that *his* prayers had been answered.

Chapter 11

Now, in the wait for a cab she went gloomy. No redness to the cheeks, no glint to the eye, no bounce to the step. Flat. Flattened by something that she said was "too real." *Too real*, she said. Too real. When she finally spoke.

In the cab she sat a polite distance from Ben in the back seat. Ben offered no details and she did not want the details anyway. She did not want to hear about it or think about it or know it; but, given her prophetic insights, she feared one day she'd read about it as she'd been reading, even in the *Voice*, about the road to Dienbienphu. ("Only" 17 American soldier/advisors were killed in Vietnam up to this moment in 1963, along with 218 wounded.) She sensed that it was only a matter of time, days, weeks, before he got the uniform and that would be the end of Ben and the beginning of the end of everything.

"Where's my sweet girl?" he said.

She also hated to be called sweet - especially at a moment like this.

"You see it, don't you," she said, staring grim-faced out the window.

"See what?" Ben said, playing innocent.

"You know."

"No I don't know."

"How it's all turned so sad."

"I don't know what you're talking about."

"I mean it's over, isn't it," she said in a voice that seemed to belong to a much older woman.

"Don't be ridiculous."

"I'm leaving. You're leaving."

Ben knew *she* was leaving, at least for a couple of weeks. But where was he going, besides the Navy? That call to arms was conditional upon another visit to the doctor, but a doctor who was said to be quite ready to overlook a trick knee here and there - as Johnston had put it to Ben with a wink. So Ben's chances were good, but there was no definite date given for his enlistment even after he passed his medical examination.

So he wasn't going anywhere, for the moment.

"Where am I going?"

"Where everybody goes," she said in a philosophical tone.

She appeared to be aging before his eyes. Certainly she had matured from virtually one moment to the next.

"Where's that?"

"Away," she said, spurning his overtures to make light of the matter. "Everybody goes away."

She repeated that three times: "Everybody goes away."

"But you're coming back," Ben said breezily, probing for some lightheartedness.

"Not for long," she said. Then, in a burst of emotion: "But I'll miss you. All of you."

He moved closer to her and tried to put an arm around her but she spurned him.

"Snap out of it, Louise. Come on."

"I'll miss Richie, you know."

Now Ben turned solemn. "I guess we had to come around to that sooner or later," he said of the taboo.

"I do love him."

"I thought you'd end up marrying him."

"We thought a lot of things this past summer. Some people thought I'd end up marrying you."

"Is this a proposal?" he laughed.

"Maybe. Why is it you never asked?"

"Like you said, that was summer..."

"And the summer's gone," she said grimly. "Now things are so complicated."

"Like what?"

"Stop playing dumb, Ben. Like you. Richie and me. Did it ever occur to you one of us has to go?"

"I never thought about it too much."

"Oh, Ben. There's three of us. Don't you and Richie ever wonder where this is going?"

"We discussed it once."

"So what happened?"

"Nothing."

"You both thought we could go along as a threesome?"

"I don't know, Louse," Ben shrugged. "I know it's unnatural, but between us..."

"Among us, Ben..."

"All right. But among us it all seemed so normal."

There was silence as she paused to reflect upon a reverie. She had been "Richie's girl" but fell for Ben the instant she spotted him posted by the door of the Bitter End. Bitter End doormen always attracted the groupies, but Ben, standing there so regally detached, was in a class by himself.

As per ritual, Richie hooked up with Ben at the Bitter End after both were done their work around one, sometimes two in the morning and they'd saunter over to the Hip Bagel where the other night owls were congregated. It was there that Lenny Bruce made the observation: "Isn't it strange how America punishes homosexuals? By locking them up with other men." Louise was already seated over a cup of espresso, sitting there happily waiting for her man.

That was Richie. Then she began making eyes at Ben and while Richie table-hopped, that one time, she whispered to Ben, "I've got a mad crush on you."

That's how it began, and it had been so much fun that they forgot the rule that three's a crowd. Anyway, this was 1963, and this was the Village, the time and the place for experimentation. To be young, carefree and reckless was a summons of the times, and those were wonderful times, Louise reflected. So wonderful and so fleeting and so happy and so sad.

"It never crossed your mind that this couldn't go on forever?" Louise said in astonishment.

"You mean a threesome?" There, now he'd said the word, a word so long left unspoken.

"If it did, it just wasn't a subject for discussion."

"Well maybe now's the time," she said firmly.

"Maybe."

"I can't leave Richie like this."

"Like what?"

"Wondering how I feel about him."

"So tell him you love him."

"He knows I love him, and that I love you, too."

"Me three."

"Stop being funny, Ben. This is serious."

"I'm serious. Tell him you love him."

"Where does that leave you?" she asked tenderly, moving to him finally with some warmth.

"I'll get along."

"I worry about you, Ben,"

Ben laughed. "I don't."

"I do."

"Don't feel sorry for me, Louise."

The cab left them off near the Back Fence at the corner of Bleecker and Sullivan. The crowds that had been lined up for Cliff were mostly indoors and seated by now. But some of the crazies were out and about. King Black, the terror of the Village at six-foot four inches, the man who used to spar with Sugar Ray Robinson and who bullied every man who crossed his path, walked by them swaggering with his white chick, but gave Ben no trouble, even offered a respectful nod and sheepish grin. He had once tested Black Belt Ben, and never again. Louise knew about the incident and she now embraced Ben and said he made her feel so safe. She said she loved him. I love you so very much, she said as they stood on the corner of Bleecker and Sullivan, stood there as though they'd never be standing there again. The other crazy on the street was Lobo the Prophet dressed in his usual blanket, his white beard down to his belly. He frequented all the clubs and quoted Scriptures impromptu. Now he was quiet but at night he howled at the moon. Then there was Jimmy Bleeds. Ben saw him sweeping the front of Improv City and Ben tightened. Louise sensed the change and said that was another reason she worried about him.

She was worried about the particular day of reckoning. She was worried about what Ben might eventually do to Jimmy Bleeds. Or what Jimmy Bleeds might do to Ben. Either way she was worried. Worry, worry, worry, Ben said as he kissed her lips.

She was not worried about Richie, she said. Richie was destined to return to Connecticut where he'd grow bald, fat and become a rich corrupted lawyer, just like his daddy. These things were written, she said. Someone upstairs in heaven wrote these things down, beforehand. She did not believe in a conventionally-correct God, but there had to be somebody upstairs.

She was not worried about Cliff. Cliff had talent.

"I don't?" Ben snapped.

Oops. She implored Ben not to take it the wrong way, what she had just said.

"You just haven't found yourself," she said, "that's all," and she shuddered to think that it might be the Navy where he finally found himself. "You should write more sketches," she said.

He had already written a sketch, a famous sketch.

Louise read his thoughts and said try again, the whole world isn't Jimmy Bleeds. Then again, maybe it is. The Jimmy Bleeds have taken over, even the Village. The bad people stay. The good people leave. "Everybody goes away." She sighed.

"I got you in a bad mood," he said.

"I'll get over it. But you're a bad boy, Ben," she said as she gently brushed his hair back against a sharp November breeze and then ran a motherly palm against his cheek. "I love you, Ben, but no more surprises like that. Life's too short. Only good surprises from now on. Promise?"

"Promise."

Holding hands they approached the entrance to the Café Muse and walked in. Cliff Harris was still backstage. The tables upon which the cider was served were small and round and the people were jammed together shoulder to shoulder, but they were in high spirits in anticipation of mirth and hilarity from Cliff Harris, a.k.a. John F. Kennedy, beloved President of the United States. The lights were dimmed. Hail to the Chief was being played. It was one o'clock in the afternoon.

Chapter 12

As cliff entered to a wild standing ovation and opened to roars of approval with his usual, "Let the word go forth from heya," the real president John F. Kennedy and his party were leaving the Dallas Trade Center where Kennedy had just given a speech. The motorcade was heading for downtown Dallas where throngs had already gathered to cheer the president. The sidewalks were packed to overflowing up to the Texas School Book Depository.

There was nothing special about this visit to Dallas. As would later be reported, Kennedy's purpose in making the trip was to help settle a "family" dispute between two fellow Democrats, Gov. John Connally and the more liberal Sen. Ralph Yarborough.

In Greenwich Village and elsewhere around the nation there was always a keen interest in the president's comings and goings and the press certainly had him constantly in its sights, but this trip to Dallas was something of a detour, a non-event.

To Paul Hogan, Cliff's agent and manager, and Nate Beloff, owner of the Café Muse, each of whom had a very special, direct and personal stake in John Kennedy, something besides Kennedy was uppermost.

Seated in the back rooms of the Café Muse as Cliff was *shpritzing* away up front, his zingers drawing gales of laughter, Paul and Nate could hardly have been more miserable and subdued. They had just received word from uptown that to their thinking spelled doom to their business and to America's new culture, a culture, or rather counterculture, that the nation had embraced and upon which they had thrived.

The meeting in which Paul and Nate had a plant, really a spy, took place in the Empire State Building and had just been concluded with disastrous results. A group of top-level radio executives had met to decide America's cultural fate.

For the past year or so the airwaves from coast to coast had been filled with folk music, dominated by the likes of Bob Dylan, the Kingston Trio, Peter, Paul and Mary, Joan Baez, Judy Collins, Miriam Makeba, Pete Seeger, Harry Belafonte and a host of kindred others whose ballads were mostly expressions of protests against the love of war and the animosity between the races.

The music was poetic and decidedly political. The lyrics were intelligent and thought-provoking and uplifting and made no money for the radio stations. Some were going belly-up. The radio stations desperately needed a new wave, a trend they could take to the bank.

Radio stations were going bankrupt as sponsors refused to support and underwrite lyrics that were thought to be subversive. The suits in the Empire State Building were in a rebellious frame of mind. They had come to despise Dylan especially for his provocative "masters of war." There was a taint of socialism, even communism in such lyrics that defamed American industry.

A dispute arose among these executives as to radio's proper role in American society. Was radio the leader or the follower when it came to public taste? They decided to put the matter to a test.

Back when Elvis and rock & roll had dominated the airwaves, business was good. They were happy. The people were happy.

Then along came Dylan and the rest of them with their ballads and protests and it seemed that this was what the nation wanted, so that's what it got. Goodbye "Jailhouse Rock," hello "Blowin' in the Wind." Radio was simply following what it perceived to be a trend.

Maybe it was time to stop following and begin leading.

Rock & roll - that's where the money was. Elvis and Pat Boone were still hot but they hardly had time to polish their blue suede shoes for all the banjo-pickin' going on. Time to kill this folk singing craze - but how?

The answer (to prayer) they all agreed had just arrived only two days earlier from Liverpool, England. The Beatles had landed. Upon arrival they had been greeted by 100,000 hysterical American teenagers who knew them through such British imports as "She Loves You," "Wanna Hold Your Hand," and "Standing There," the same three recordings that had inflamed the young throughout Great Britain.

The Beatles would be broadcasting's savior. This was a calculated plan, hatched on this day, by this hour.

These four Beatles would be the Pied Pipers, it was agreed around the table in the Empire State Building, and so it was unanimously agreed to kill folk singing not by halting it, no, not at all, but rather by playing it to death, over and over again, round the clock without pause, until the nation begged never to hear "Matilda" again!

Behold, therefore, the Beatles!

The scheme worked. Folksongs would be banished after the people had their fill. This took time, several years, in fact, but gradually no more songs of protest, no more lyrics dealing with issues. Instead, virtually all pop music dealt with boy-girl themes, love sought, love found, love lost, with the Beatles at the fore.

The Beatles, in turn, begat scores of imitators and soon love turned to sex, sex to violence as succeeding groups of unruly, long-haired individuals found it necessary to play louder and harder in order to keep up or to stay ahead of the trend.

Though still wildly popular, the Beatles were being surpassed. They were becoming rather quaint compared to groups whose hair was longer, whose beat was stronger and whose lyrics introduced the love of drugs and violence. Drugs and violence thus became synonymous with rock & roll. Rock & roll evolved into rock, rock into hard rock, hard rock into heavy metal. On stage clothes were ripped and guitars were smashed as an expression of mindless rage. The sex act was simulated to the frenzied delight of thousands who were beginning to forget the Beatles' tender supplication - "I Wanna Hold Your Hand."

At this point, Paul Hogan and Nate Beloff only knew this; rock & roll was here to stay. The ballad form of appeal to togetherness was doomed. No more calls for brotherhood. No more sweetness. No more tenderness. As Paul Hogan and Nate Beloff had it figured, rage, this was to become the nation's wine of sorrow and bread of affliction. Yes, love was out. Rage was in.

Chapter 13

Howard Penny was there, as he had promised Cliff he would be, but he was not laughing at Cliff's zingers, like the rest of them were, all 200 of them down here in the darkened Café Muse basement theater; 200 and maybe more, as many as could be packed in sitting and standing, howling at every line and lusting for more, as much Kennedy as Cliff could provide.

No, Howie was not laughing. He was high on some shit that some stranger had given him, some cat cruising Washington Park Square in a pimpmobile, and that was a lesson. Never accept gifts from strangers. This was supposed to be cocaine mixed with something else and it was that something else that had Howie so troubled. The room kept moving on him and he could not get Cliff into focus up there on stage.

The fuzz also had him troubled. He kept thinking about the fuzz. Some were his friends. They know his habit but they also knew they could count on him for information. Not that he was an informer; he was just being reliable. That was all his dad out there in Tulsa asked of him.

He'd never be a doctor like his dad, or an English professor like his mom, or, scrawny and awkward as he was as athletic and as fucking all-American as were his two younger brothers; so least he could do, said his dad upon discovering that his eldest was a dope addict - least you can be is reliable. Meanwhile, his dad said, going back a couple of years, get the hell out of this house! You belong in Greenwich Village.

Yes sir!

And he kept his word. He was being reliable. When the fuzz came along with questions, he answered. Even when they did not ask, he answered. For example, Richie and the snake. Then Richie without that snake. Then all the headlines about that uptown dude who was bitten to death by a snake.

Howie put two and two together and made the call to the Sixth Precinct. He named Richie. He liked Richie but Richie had everything, mostly chicks, the chicks he never shared. Always it was Richie and Ben, Ben and Richie, and all he could do is tag along. Mr. Invisible.

They never asked for him, never included him - and only he, Howard Penny had once roomed with Lenny Bruce. That ought to count for something.

The fuzz were grateful when he named Richie and even more grateful when he told them that Richie used to live up there on 82nd with the very same guy who'd been bitten to death. That was good information, good enough to get them to question Gloria MacKenzie earlier in the day and to question Richie himself now, this very minute.

That's why Richie wasn't here for Cliff. Richie was being interrogated.

Being friends with the fuzz could only help. Otherwise long ago they'd have bagged Howie and shipped him off to the Tombs for trafficking in shit and for his association with such undesirables as Dr. Dreck who peddled coke and now heroin to the young.

Jimmy Bleeds, who also did some trafficking, was another valued friend because of his underworld connections, though as of late Howie was on the outs with Jimmy. And that was not a desirable thing.

Howie had assured Jimmy Bleeds that Ben Jaffa would make no fuss about being ripped off for fear of being deported, Howie forgetting that Ben Jaffa was a bona fide citizen of the United States of America. But in any case, Ben Jaffa was being confrontational about the whole thing, so Jimmy Bleeds was furious at Howie for such bad information and Howie made sure to step aside when he and Jimmy Bleeds happened to be sharing the same Bleecker Street sidewalk. Jimmy Bleeds had a habit of staring, or rather glaring at people who got on his bad side and it was always the other person who blinked first. Even when he was high on shit and kept teetering from one corner to next, Howie was alert enough to sense trouble, and Jimmy Bleeds was trouble.

Life in a big pond like New York was not easy for an ugly duckling like Howard Penny. Howie lived by his wits. He survived by knowing all the secrets and by making himself useful by judiciously dishing out such information. He was a tag-along but he watched and he listened.

By watching and listening, for example, he knew that Ben was *shtupping* Louise in the ladies' room at the Village Gate while Richie was waiting tables, and when he reported this to Richie, Richie told him to fuck off. "Geez," Richie had sneered, "you're so transparent."

Okay, so now who's crying? Now who's being *transparent*? Now who's being interrogated?

The fuzz that Howie feared were not the uniformed boys from the Sixth. They were friends, mostly. But the two who had stopped him right before he got here to the Café Muse were no friends. He'd never seen them before. They were in plain clothes and all they showed him was a badge that said something like FBI. They were Feds.

They kept asking him if he knew anything subversive. They did not care about drugs. That was a concern for the local authorities. Subversiveness, that was Federal. Cliff Harris, was he subversive? Lenny Bruce? Didn't you room with that *prevert*? They kept saying *pre-vert* and how these preverts were poisoning America with the language they were using.

Lenny Bruce was a *prevert*. A drug addict and a *prevert*.

Howie, who still had a soft spot for Lenny, said Lenny took drugs because he was afraid of being assassinated. That's why he was a drug addict. He was paranoid and was convinced that he was number one on the CIA hit list.

Interesting, said the two Feds. (Because it may have been true.)

About Cliff Harris - where did his material come from? Was he a foreign agent? Was he taking orders from Moscow?

People think he's the president, you know. Maybe he's funny but people take him seriously and if he ever talked like that *prevert* Lenny Bruce the repercussions could be awful. Because people think it's JFK talking.

If Cliff Harris gets too funny and starts with the kind of talk that's been going around about overthrowing the government, you will let us know. Howie said sure. Terrific, said the two Feds. We're counting on you.

All that had happened only moments before when all the people were outside waiting to get in, and Howie was still spooked. The Feds had also brought up Cliff's runaway bestselling album, "Thank You, Mr. President."

That takeoff on the First Family had the country in stitches. But was the humor really harmless?

I don't know, said Howie.

We're checking it out, said the two Feds.

Howie, still unable to focus on Cliff up there on stage, was now thinking that he might keep himself on Cliff's good side by sharing the news about his being under surveillance, except that Cliff knew that already. But it could not hurt to tell him anyway. Couldn't hurt to have friends. Too bad about Richie.

Chapter 14

Richie Bell never thought it would come to this, but he was homesick. *Home cooking.* Even that you had to eat in a restaurant. After leaving Gloria MacKenzie's apartment he went over to Katz's Deli on Houston for some pastrami and Katz's Deli, this day, was full of *tourists!* Probably filling up for showtime at the Café Muse. The locals that he used to like to sit and chat with were someplace but not here; *Cleveland* - they were here from table to table, and they were loud, as if they belonged.

That was a bad sign. The squares were taking over. As he walked back to Sullivan to get showered and changed for Cliff's matinee he was alert to the grainy and grimy side of Greenwich Village as never before. Squares, cops and bums. The streets were filthy and empty with beer cans and liquor bottles, noisy with nut cases like Dr. Blast and King Black and Lobo the Prophet yelling to no one and everyone in broad daylight, smelly with vomit. Squalor, strangeness and derangement. That's what he saw. That was all he saw. Up to now he had been blind to all that, being so caught up in the romance of the Bohemian scene - and being sated with Louise Carmen.

The same Louise Carmen who thought she owed her old boyfriend in Wheeling a debt and saw nothing wrong in paying it off. He could not figure it out. Was love so perishable? Was devotion so fragile? Was sex so cheap? Were all women like that?

Maybe, he was thinking, it was time to call it a summer, call it an autumn, call it quits, pack up and go back home, not to Harvard - forget school, he'd never make it as a square lawyer - but to Hartford. Sally Caruthers was the-girl-next-door and Sally was waiting. He had left her waiting until he was finished with the Village, which he figured meant stardom as a folksinger. Then, since that was far from   happening, he figured to stay until Louise Carmen came around and agreed to marry him. That was even further from happening.

So perhaps it was Sally who was meant to be. He missed her. Suddenly he missed her. Surely she was not like that, cheap, fragile and perishable. Sally was down-home and her love for him had been true since grad school. Since kindergarten! She phoned him periodically to remind him that she was still waiting, would always be waiting.

She was rooting for him and would be by his side no matter what he chose for a career, the law or the guitar. Made no difference to her. But come back, she said. He assured her that he would, and then forgot about her.

But now he was not forgetting. He was remembering how good life had been in Hartford. The table there had been set for him. From the richness of his upbringing he had grown into manhood strong, sure, confident and carefree. He had overcome TB and asthma and laughed when he had been warned to quit smoking. He laughed at pretty much everything.

Even now he saw the humor of his situation; whimpering over a girl. Hadn't his dad taught him to love 'em and leave 'em and hadn't he done just that from one fling to the next? But this was different. Louise was different.

Approaching the apartment - and he'd never call it a *pad* since the slang had already gone mainstream - he decided to change moods; it was out of character anyway for him to remain sullen. All was not lost. Adventures were still ahead. Fun was still to be had. There was no telling what might happen from one instant to the next.

He was sold on this place and he had even partially sold his parents on it when he told them Eleanor Roosevelt used to live in Greenwich Village. Anybody who was anybody used to live in Greenwich Village.

When he got to the apartment he found it empty at a time when they'd usually still be asleep were it not for Cliff Harris getting them up and out so early this morning, and that's where they all were at this moment, at the Café Muse. He ought to be there, too, he was thinking. He'd lost track of time, but that was typical. He carried no watch because who cared what time it was! He'd be late for Cliff but here, in the Village, there was no such thing as being late. If you showed up, you showed up, if you didn't, you didn't. That's what made the Village so perfect for Richie.

Life was not something you pursued. Wait long enough and it would catch up. If it didn't, just as well.

Besides, nothing was really *important*. If the phone rang, Richie seldom picked it up. When the mail came, Richie seldom checked it out. For weeks now, letters had been forwarded to him from the Selective Service Administration, the draft board, and he figured to get around to opening the envelopes sooner or later if at all.

The apartment, Richie noticed, was not only empty of people, but also of things. No guitar. That depressed him momentarily. He'd get another one. But the reason he smashed it brought Louise to mind. Well, he thought, he'd lay on the charm before she left and if that failed to snap her back to her senses, he'd get her in the end regardless.

97

When it came to girls, he never lost. True, Louise was eluding him, but the chase was exhilarating, confounding as it was. She was something, that Louise. She was not simply another chick. Chicks he had all over the place. He called them out-of-town tryouts. But Louise was Broadway!

After he showered he searched for his clothes. The closet was nearly empty. Howie again! Howie trading in clothes to the Army and Navy shop on McDougal to get cash for stash. This happened time and again and there was no proof. But it had to be Howie.

Ben would be most upset. He could not afford a new wardrobe. For the time being Richie had one or two outfits left to make do for this afternoon. But what a pisser was that Howie! No wonder Lenny had kicked him out.

Richie laughed thinking about Howie. He laughed thinking of Ben. No it wasn't funny but it was funny how every man played his part according to type. Howie was a little prick and everything he did conformed and confirmed. Ben was royalty, but he had no clothes. What choice was there but to laugh?

The doorbell rang. Richie was in no hurry to answer. Whoever it was could wait, or leave.

Now he shaved and was beginning to feel like his old self. No, he thought, going back home was not an option. He had changed too much to go back. It was the same for everybody who had had a taste of the Village life.

You could never be the same again. Now you dressed differently. You spoke differently and you even thought differently. What you once thought was good was now bad and what you once thought was bad was now good. Wrong was right and right was wrong.

You drank espresso for coffee, you smoked Gaulois for Camels, you got high instead of drunk, you played chess for tennis, you traded in Sinatra for Dylan, Willie Mays for Jack

Kerouac, your friends were white, black, gay and lesbian and you were protesting against everything that was square.

Instead of a gun, the guitar and banjo were your weapons of choice. Rather than football, you attended hootenannies. Instead of midnight panty raids you were up till morning debating socialism versus democracy, Hegel versus Spinoza. Sartre and Kierkegaard were bigger than Mantle and Mays.

You were both ahead of your time and behind the times. You were the real America and you were the exiled America. You were the new flag America turned to and you were the scapegoat. You were the nation's pride and you were the nation's shame.

No, there was no turning back.

Such distinctions between then and now came to life when Richie's parents arrived one day unexpected and unannounced and it was the day when everybody was cohabitating. (With virile Jack Kennedy in office and libertine Hugh Hefner ruling the culture, fucking was in. Under Eisenhower there'd been no fucking in America.) This was not an orgy as there was no trading partners. An orgy was likewise something planned and here these things just happened. Richie answered the door wearing only his boxer shorts, two naked girls draped on either side of him.

His mother gasped and ran back to the car. His dad gave the room a reproachful once-over, and he too ran back to the safety of his car and Connecticut. Later he wrote: "We love you, son. But it's time to stop the bullshit. Time to get down to the business of life. What about Harvard? What about Sally? You've had your fling. Now it's time to come home."

The doorbell, that's what made him think that it may be his parents again. Instead two uniformed police officers were staring him in the face, Officers DeVito and Toscano.

Just a couple of questions, they said, as Richie, casual and composed, said he was in a hurry to get to the Café Muse.

We know what's going on there, said the officers, and we will not keep you, but...

They questioned him about his snake and about his roommate Timothy Baines. Richie was cooperative and responsive. He had nothing to hide. Yes the snake was his and no, he had not left it behind to be with Tim, and how it got back there, this he did not know. Except that Tim had been a constant visitor here, and maybe, as a prank, decided to steal it, as, quite frankly, he and Tim were on the outs over a dispute that was too involved to go into at this time.

The officers listened intently and politely. Still seemed strange, they said, how the snake got back to 82nd Street. The prank theory sounded outlandish. Wasn't Timothy Baines afraid of snakes?

At first, yes, but eventually I got him used to it, Richie said.

Still seems farfetched, said the officers. Most people are leery of these crawling creatures. Tough to imagine a guy just learning about snakes having the guts to haul one back to his own apartment.

Then you'd have to have known Tim, said Richie. Tim was capable of great vengeance and there was a moment in our relationship when he would have done anything to distress me - and he knew how much I loved the snake.

So why wouldn't he have simply thrown it into the river? Why take it home?

Richie had no response for that except to repeat that you had to have known Timothy Baines. The guy was mean and vindictive and mean and vindictive people are not easy to figure out.

Officer DeVito arched an eyebrow and said that that explanation would have to do for now. But this was not necessarily the end of the investigation so would Richie please make himself available if more questions were forthcoming.

Any time, said Richie.

He was still unfazed after they left. He was pleased, in fact, to be in the middle of a caper. It was another adventure, another story to share with the gang at the Hip Bagel. Good for a laugh.

Now he was ready to join the world at the Café Muse.

Yes it was the world. At the very least it was the center of the American universe. America revolved around the Greenwich Village. Greenwich Village revolved around Bleecker Street. Bleecker Street revolved around the Café Muse when Cliff was in session. So this was the place. That's how Richie had it figured when he entered the jammed basement 1:30 in the afternoon, though he didn't know what time it was, nor that at precisely this moment three shots rang out in Dallas, Texas.

Chapter 15

Cliff was zipping along and only those who knew him recognized the absence of enthusiasm in his sketches. He was going through the motions, faking it, phoning it in, according to the show biz slang. The people did not know that they were getting but half a John Kennedy and half a Cliff Harris. As long as he kept up the Kennedyesque patter accompanied by the Kennedy mannerisms and the Kennedy vocal inflections - as long as he did all that they were satisfied; thrilled, actually.

The skit where he's serenading "Jackie" on her birthday with his rendition of the ditty "Roses are Red" drew wails of laughter. Adopting the Kennedyesque plainsong monotone, Cliff proceeded with, "Roses-are-ah red-ah, violets are-ah blue, sugah is-ah sweet my-ya love, and-ah, show are you. Now let us go fo-wawd and-ah blow out the-ah candles." That was the show stopper; but then, everything was. "No Bobby (the president's brother and attorney general who was even younger and younger-looking than Jack and thus the object of raillery about still being so wet behind the ears), you can't lick-ah icing off the-ah cake."

The mask, however, would soon be coming off, if all went according to plan, as Cliff was preparing to surprise them by switching to that sick routine, the *sick shtick*, that had   Kennedy trading missiles with Khrushchev, Kennedy almost gladly offering up American cities for annihilation.

Wipe out Philadelphia? Why not? They're all Negros! San Francisco? Take it Nikita. They're all queers. Lenny Bruce material - only many perilous steps ahead. In other words he was going to zing them with a grotesque Kennedy and thus, in his view, awaken them from their slumber.

Forget the beatific stuff; here comes the ugly truth. Not necessarily the truth about Kennedy, but the truth about themselves, ourselves, that other America, the Nixon America that was slouching in the wings.

Cliff's intention - and his intentions were well-meant - was to hold up a mirror that reflected an America with all its blemishes. The roundtable at McSorely's had actually dissuaded him from going ahead with the plan, he was fully prepared to drop it, but then he saw them out there and was provoked.

This was the time to reveal himself as Cliff Harris, a Cliff Harris with a message, a Cliff Harris with a prophecy. The prophecy being that given the right moment, the right leader, or rather the wrong moment, the wrong leader, we are all vulnerable to thuggery and bestiality. The line between civility and barbarism was as fragile as the frail gap between Beethoven and Hitler.

(Lest we forget Salem and McCarthyism and what we did to the Indians.)

Cliff did not have to go far to discover the ugliness that was percolating in all of us. He only had to look inside himself. He did not like what he saw. Since it was true, according to the wisdom of the fathers, that each individual is an entire universe, therefore he, Cliff Harris, was no better and no worse than the rest, and when he was good, that is, when he was Kennedy, he was very good, and when he was bad, that is, when he was himself and raging under the influence of alcohol or perceived injustice, he was very bad.

So it was not much of a philosophical leap for Cliff to jump from the specific to the general as a judgment of human nature.

First to provoke him this afternoon were the cameras he saw out there from the three major networks, their lights and their scampering up and down the aisles distracting him and breaking his rhythm. Time and again he had warned Gloria MacKenzie and Nate Beloff that he'd never go on if the cameras showed up.

But here they were, no doubt because his "Thank You, Mr. President" album had shot to the top of the charts and thus Cliff Harris was no longer merely entertainment; he was news!

He had always been news but never more so than this moment and when the networks came calling, neither Nate or Gloria or a team of elephants could stop them - not TV. There was no stopping TV. TV was the elephant.

As if the cameras weren't enough, out there mixed among Mr. and Mrs. America were the damned Soviets, the KGB, who tried to blend in but stuck out like corpses among the living for being so stiff and uncoordinated.

Cliff counted four of them monitoring him this afternoon and it did not take much to spot them.

They were the ones who did not laugh. Or laughed at the wrong times. As always, they were here for inside information, under the delusion that he, Cliff, had a pipeline to the White House.

So wherever Cliff went, they were sure to go. When first sighting them, after the Bay of Pigs, tensions high, Cliff was spooked. Then after Kennedy and Khrushchev had a flare-up in Vienna, Kennedy returning a chastened man, Cliff was merely indulgent.

Now he came to expect them and was almost glad to see them. It meant he was still hot, as was Kennedy, as was everything from the Berlin Wall, to the Soviet's playing the China card (which concerned the United States), to America's increasing involvement in Vietnam (which concerned the Soviet Union).

They followed Cliff from crisis to crisis and maybe, Cliff figured, they wanted to be recognized as a reminder to Cliff and to the president himself that Khrushchev was listening.

Khrushchev was listening all right and didn't get the joke. What joke? The Cold War was at its height. Despite the East-West treaty banning atomic testing everywhere but underground, the world was a jittery place, fretful that the leaders of the two Great Powers might arrive at a misunderstanding that could wipe out the world.

So while gallows humor was partly acceptable, personal insults were seen as grave and dire affronts.

The KGB boys out there taking notes squirmed each time Cliff let out a zinger that touched their leader.

On being informed that jokes were being told in America at his expense, gags about his being corpulent and boorish, Khrushchev was livid. He sent letters not to Cliff but directly to the White House warning the president that such levity could come with a price. Such personal attacks were reckless. Especially wisecracks that involved his wife. These "jokes" were not only tasteless but an affront to Russian womanhood as a whole.

These jokes - coming from the president's look-alike and sound-alike - could lead to war!

Letters were sent back to the effect that, to begin with, the jokes were not Kennedy's. They came from an entertainer, a comedian who made his livelihood by *impersonating* the president. Secondly, in the United States there was a thing called FREEDOM OF SPEECH, which prevented even the president from muzzling a citizen.

What's more, Dear Mr. Khrushchev, contrary to the prevailing belief, here and abroad, this impersonator Cliff Harris does not speak for the president. His scripts are all his own and are not, Mr. Khrushchev, sanctioned by the White House.

Lies! said Khrushchev. Why in his country jokes had to be approved in advance. Never mind freedom of speech. We're talking the bogus cry of fire in a crowded theater.

As an aside from one world leader to another, Khrushchev declared that never would he, Khrushchev, allow himself to be so caricatured by a so-called impersonator, and even if he relented concerning his own person, he would forbid any such performer from engaging in ridicule against the President of the United States, given these troubled times and the skittishness between the two Great Powers.

He certainly would forbid any such diatribes against the lovely First Lady of America. In the Soviet Union, Khrushchev continued, humor was the sugar-coated face of truth, therefore it stood to reason that this "humor" forthcoming from Cliff Harris was really a reflection of the president's personal views - and this was insulting and very dangerous.

When the hotline was hooked up between Washington and Moscow, Khrushchev took to the phone 11 frenetic times within a period of eight months to complain about Cliff Harris' ongoing insolence.

Kennedy laughed. He swore that he could do nothing to stop his copycat. Kennedy being Kennedy, he even hinted that he was amused by Cliff and did not mind being the object of harmless levity and sport.

But even the president did not have the final word - even in his own backyard there were spooks, which consisted of the FBI and the CIA, two organizations that were about as lighthearted as the KGB.

Agents from the FBI, and CIA, and the Secret Service were likewise on Cliff's trail. They were also here today. On reading the briefs, Kennedy was said to howl at Cliff's gags, and along the same reasoning he seldom missed a Cliff Harris performance on the Ed Sullivan show. There was a rumor that he planned to visit the Café Muse to catch a personal glimpse of his much-celebrated and much-maligned impersonator. That came close to happening the week before when Kennedy was in town and only blocks away from Greenwich Village.

That word had some validity, but another rumor, entirely implausible, had it that Kennedy had opted to postpone his visit to Dallas, since he had no appetite for Democratic infighting, and had instead proposed a visit to the Café Muse for this very Friday, November 22. That would all come out later as specious backtracking and second guessing, yet talk of conspiracies and prophesies of assassination were quite legitimate and real. A month *earlier*, in October, the esteemed Arthur Krock of *The New York Times* intimated that President Kennedy's life was at risk and that if an assassination attempt were to take place, it would be the work of the CIA. Krock reported that he got that information from a high government source. Krock and Kennedy were close friends, often had lunch together, and it has been suggested that Krock's unnamed source was the president himself.

Once in a while these spooks came out of the shadows and approached Cliff directly. Cordially, they represented themselves as members of the Administration and asked Cliff if he could tone down his remarks about leaders overseas.

Hey, we don't care how you portray the president, they said.

The president can take a joke. He enjoys a good laugh. He thinks you're a riot. But those guys, you know, like Khrushchev, hell, they take this stuff seriously.

So did Cliff, except that *he* objected to being the target of so much fantasy. He had every right to be paranoid and even gloomily remarked that one time at the Hip Bagel - "one false move and I start World War fucking Three!"

As if being hounded from both sides weren't enough, he was once approached to turn *traitor*! Inferences - said this garlic-smelling character - can be drawn that you are critical of the United States and its president, Mr. Harris. If you would take your act to Moscow and speak out against capitalism and the undeniable rise of communism, you will be accorded the laurels of a hero. "Who the fuck sent you?" Cliff said, escorting the man by the collar. "Has to be Lenny!"

No it wasn't Lenny, but on the business of being hounded by all manner of fuzz, Cliff and Lenny were partners.

Lenny Bruce had confided to Cliff that sometimes it got so bad that when he peered beyond the footlights of the Café Au Go Go he imagined nothing but fuzz out there in the audience. (This was not always his imagination.) Cliff knew the feeling, and he even knew the fact. During the night of a blizzard in 1962 nobody showed up at the Café Muse, nobody except the spooks, and that night he was indeed performing for an audience of fuzz.

So the spooks were here again this afternoon, but where was Lenny? Cliff eyed the tables one by one. No signs of his idol and that too was a distraction; yet another reason his delivery was going out so flat - so flat that he could hear his own voice, a sure sign, to him, that he was bombing. They were laughing, but he was bombing.

Lenny was an inspiration and only Lenny's approval counted. Lenny had the guts to say "nigger, wop, spic" up there on stage as a means to diminish the power of those vulgarities. Say those words often enough, Lenny proclaimed, and they lose their wallop.

Only Lenny had such guts, and it was Lenny who had accused Cliff of being so "fakate mainstream," doling out chewing gum for the brain to docile college students and Kennedy-starved burghers. While he, Cliff, kept cranking out the same harmless send-ups about the Peace Corps, Lenny was *out there*, like this:

"You know what a Jew is; one who killed our Lord. We did it two thousand years ago, and there should be a statute of limitations for that crime. Why should we Jews pay these dues? Granted we killed him and he was a nice guy; although there was even some talk that we didn't kill Christ, we killed the one on the left. But I confess that we killed him, despite those who said that Roman soldiers did it.

"Yes we did. My family. I found a note in my basement: 'We killed him - signed Morty.'"

Lenny Bruce was a Jew who asked that Christians and Jews for once act like Christ, and for that reason, he told Cliff, he was going to dedicate his autobiography to Christ (which he did) as follows: I dedicate this book to all the followers of Christ and his teaching; in particular to a true Christian - Jimmy Hoffa - because he hired ex-convicts as, I assume, Christ would have.

Lenny named his work-in-progress autobiography "How to Talk Dirty and Influence People," and he refused Cliff's help in providing a *goyishe* perspective on the grounds that Cliff had talent but no soul. That stung.

Soul! That's what Cliff was preparing to give the people this afternoon soon after he satisfied their lust for Camelot, and it was only a matter of what to start with - the women who chased Cliff and demanded the golden shower so that they could say that the "president" had pissed on them? The women who asked to be whipped by the "president?"

Or what about the woman who claimed that she had had a longstanding adulterous affair with the president and was jilted not by Jack, but by the president's father, Joe, who gave her half a million dollars to disappear. She took the money and where did she run? To Cliff Harris. On the rebound she wanted Cliff as the next best thing. He declined, of course. Not only was this perverse, but traitorous. But she was here for his every performance - even today - gazing at Cliff through eyes of hurtful longing. What did that say?

These were no whores who made those advances, but Main Street, middle American women, who proved that it wasn't all Ozzie and Harriet out there from sea to shining sea! The people had a right to know that there was sickness in the land. There was also McNamara and his gang who were lusting for war and drawing maps of Vietnam. All was mostly quiet on the campus front but blacks and whites were at each other's throats.

Cliff was determined to let go with all that in addition to his *sick shtick* about Kennedy and Khrushchev trading bombs - but first he wanted Lenny to be here and bear witness to a Cliff Harris with soul.

Ironically, out there in the audience Cliff thought he spotted Honey, Lenny's blonde Venus. She seldom showed up for Lenny. Lenny was wild about her but there was always something going on between them and it drove Lenny nuts to be so unrequited.

Cliff likewise knew the meaning of unrequited, and even at this moment as he was *shpritzing* along he was haunted by the flashback. Melanie Atherton of Philadelphia's Main Line had been the love of his life and she dumped him for a doctor. She was a socialite with beauty and brains who had spurned millionaires to see Cliff through thin and thin - as she put it with a smile. She was a headstrong girl but gave Cliff nothing but tenderness. She had been in love with Cliff throughout his struggles to the top and precisely when he made it to the top she said fame and show biz were not for her. Her defection shattered him and he kept searching for her as well beyond the footlights. One day, he thought, she'd show up, and on that day he'd quit drinking, even quit show biz. He had offered as much and it still wasn't enough, or rather too late.

She had faithfully sat through all his Philadelphia auditions and she adored him most of all when he failed. She was always there to comfort and console him and he had counted on her to be there for the rest of his days. When he turned Kennedy - when success swamped him - she ducked and said goodbye.

Thus fate had given him Jack but not Jackie. Fate had also given him a bad back just like Jack's only Cliff's affliction was not the result of heroics on PT-109, but came from a beating at the hands of Eddie "Fedora" Gallanter after Cliff declined to give up the Café Muse in favor of Gallanter's uptown nightclub - at twice the pay.

Cliff was in constant pain.

He was having a miserable time up there on stage. Maybe it was the time of day that was at fault. He was a night person and had never performed when the sun was out. He did not like daylight, when everything was so real and so harshly exposed. Maybe that's why he was now so open to an avalanche of troubled reverie. But despite all these demons distracting him throughout his performance, he had them in his pocket.

Now, adopting Shelley Berman's *shtick* of using a phantom telephone as a prop, Cliff, still half-hearted, smoothed into the routine that always snagged them: "Dean? Dean Rusk! This is the ah-president. Listen, Dean. Yes it's urgent. No it's not about Cuber. No, it's not about Castro. Jackie wants to know if you-ah can-ah babysit for-ah John-John."

That sent them into convulsions. This was happening downtown at 1:40 p.m. Uptown at this same moment CBS-TV had interrupted the soap opera *As the World Turns* for Walter Cronkite's report that the President of the United States had been shot and was "seriously wounded."

Chapter 16

Cliff's Big Three, his cabinet of Paul Hogan, Nate Beloff, and Gloria MacKenzie, respectively agent, café owner, and café manager, were seated in Gloria's office as Gloria, a procession of cigarettes dangling from the side of her mouth, counted the box office take and a good take it was.

The phone rang and Paul Hogan picked it up, listened, hung up and, ashen-faced said: "Man claims there's a bomb in the house."

Gloria stopped counting, gazed up at Paul as if he'd said nothing of importance, and resumed counting. Nate the constant worrier, with wrinkles to show it, a man who always waited for the other shoe to drop, threw up his arms horror-stricken and began to pace.

"You'll wear out the carpet," said Gloria as she sorted the bills in piles.

"Gloria," said Paul. "Did you hear what I said?"

"You mean we've never had bomb scares before?"

"But you never know," said Nate, his grieving eyes showing the pain of the moment, and the years.

"You men are such babies," Gloria snickered in her throaty gin-soaked voice. She'd had three husbands and each in his own way taught her intolerance for the opposite sex. "We've had bomb scares before, we'll have them again. Comes with the territory."

"Some territory," said Paul Hogan, who, as Cliff's agent, guardian and babysitter, was beginning to feel punch-drunk.

"We've got to..." Nate began, but Gloria cut him short.

"We've got to do nothing," she said, wrapping the money in rubber bands. "The show goes on."

"We did have something just like this two Friday's ago," said Paul, coming around to Gloria's point of view.

"That's when the album first came out," sighed Nate. "What's the excuse today?"

"The world is full of crazies," said Gloria. "Is this news to you, Nate?"

"But shouldn't we call the police?" said Nate.

"Call the police?" said Paul. "Outside there's nothing but police."

"So shouldn't we tell them?"

"Nobody's telling nothing to nobody," said Gloria, now smoking and chewing gum at the same time. There was an evil glint to her grin from watching the boys squirm. She was not evil, but *somebody* had to wear the pants around here, she was thinking.

"We owe it to the people and to Cliff," Nate protested submissively.

"I think Nate's right," said Paul.

"We should make an announcement," said Nate.

"Do you hear what's going on out there? Cliff hurting them?" said Gloria. "You boys ever hear of *timing*?"

"I say we make an announcement right now. I don't want to be responsible for a catastrophe," said Nate.

"Right now, Nate?" said Gloria sarcastically.

"Right now."

"I agree," said Paul, swinging back to Nate.

"That'll only start a stampede," said Gloria. "Is that what you boys want?"

Paul Hogan sighed. "I wish we'd never made that album. It just made everything worse."

"Worse?" laughed Gloria.

"You know what he means," said Nate.

"He means success is too much of a good thing. Not to me it isn't," said Gloria. "Suits me just fine."

"What he means," said Nate, "is that he can't handle all the *dreck* that comes along with success," said Nate.

Nate couldn't handle all the dreck, either, and the dreck started to fall with the release two Friday's back of Cliff's "Thank You, Mr. President" album. Copies of the album vanished from the stores before the truckers had a chance to unload them.

Lines going back a mile formed throughout Manhattan's record shops. The people grew frantic when the Sold Out signs went up. They rioted for a mere glimpse of the cover, which showed Cliff Harris (John Kennedy) playing touch football with actors portraying (and resembling) Jackie, Bobby and Ethel. Loudspeakers broadcasting the album's contents were mounted outside the record shops to appease the mobs before new shipments arrived.

United LP, heretofore, small potatoes in the recording industry, was compelled to press another 100,000 copies overnight, and then another 100,000 (altogether up to seven million copies, a new all-time high for LP's until the Beatles come along) to meet the nationwide demand.

The frenzy caught everybody off-guard. Paul Hogan and Nate Beloff at first rejoiced upon the news of their hit, but on beholding the madness on the streets of America, they plunged into despair. Beginning two weeks ago, people who couldn't buy the album for its scarcity were threatening to march on Café Muse and tear it apart. Bomb threats followed, particularly from over-patriotic Americans who thought the album contained subversive material, material insulting to the First Family and the nation. There was a rumor that Cliff Harris as John Kennedy had made a remark that suggested Jackie was having an affair with Aristotle Onassis. Extra police from the Sixth Precinct were quartered at virtually every Village intersection.

Then, as the album became available in huge quantities and both lovers and haters of the Kennedys were sated, the commotion died down, and the bomb threats stopped - only to be revived again today.

"He's only got another hour of material left," said Gloria. "*Then* we clear everybody out."

Gloria's reasoning had nothing to do with macho - though macho she was. This was all business. Get the word out, especially with the networks here today, that the Café Muse was vulnerable to bomb threats and out goes the hard-earned money and glory. The people would stay home.

For it wasn't only Cliff who got the limelight. She shared it as well. On account of Cliff she was a woman of power. Same for all of Greenwich Village. With Cliff - Cliff and his pipeline into mainstream America - all that glitter, all the excitement would be gone, too.

Greenwich Village would soon lose its title as the culture-leader of America. She, then, would have lost everything, for her life was a shell. She had nothing but this club. She had no man but Richie Bell and of Richie she had but a half, if that much.

But better half of Richie than all of her past husbands put together. She still had the scars from their beatings, one an insurance salesman, another a Society polo player, the third a poet. She sure knew how to pick 'em!

Eight years ago the poet Meredith Stillwell swept her off her middle class feet, from out there on Long Island, and plunked her down in Greenwich Village to live among the Beats. The Beats, Kerouac and company, were the precursors of the Beatniks and were perhaps the last true Bohemians. Gloria, intellectual by nature, was in love with the scene and in love with Stillwell. She waited tables downtown and washed floors uptown as Stillwell wrote his touching poems of love, brotherhood and faithfulness. In real life he was violent, and a two-timer. Gloria, a product of the passive 1950's, thought his tantrums and beatings were all her fault. She deserved to be battered, and she owed him everything, particularly this new stimulating life. He had saved her from obscurity of housewifery.

The day she caught him *flagrante delicto* something snapped and she was meek no more.

To this day people talk about the thrashing she gave Stillwell in broad daylight on Bleecker Street. Traffic stopped, pedestrians gawked as she punched and kicked until she had him down crying uncle.

This was the turning point for Gloria MacKenzie. From that moment on she was much feared in the Village and even the toughest uptown bargainers approached her with care when talking deals at the Café Muse. Nate Beloff had hired her simply because he was afraid not to.

But she was not nearly as tough as all that. She was unwavering only as concerned the talent, insisting that anyone who appeared in her club desist from engagements elsewhere for a period of 12 months.

When she hired an act she declared: "Now I own you." There was too much horse-trading as it was among the clubs, making for far too many feuds and rivalries - as was the case between Cliff Harris and Eddie "Fedora" Gallanter.

When she said "I own you" she only meant that this was a risky business, that virtually 10 out of 10 performers never made it, but if by some fluke one of them did, she wanted to be there collecting on her investment.

One such talent, a folksinger from Iowa, forgot the arrangement and signed with the Café Dijon. Nate Beloff threatened to sue. Gloria had no patience for such niceties and instead broke into the fellow's act the third night of his betrayal and pulled him off stage by the ears. Some call it the best show the Café Dijon ever put on. That incident stamped her reputation as Tough As Nails Gloria. But even her rivals and detractors had to concede that she had a keen eye for talent.

As for her love life - Stillwell had taken care of any romantic notions that remained in her heart. The male gender, to her thinking, fell into two categories, boys or brutes. Only Richie Bell was a *man* and he was easy to love because she could not have him.

Her sense of humor, her soft side, she showed only to a select few. She no longer believed in art and music, in artists and musicians, as redemption to herself and her world. What others saw as a "movement" she saw as a passing fancy. What others saw as a lost generation she saw as a found generation, a generation that had been found by the rich and the spoiled.

To be truly hip meant to be part of nothing. (J.D. Salinger, Ayn Rand, Simone de Beauvoir were her heroes.) When others called it a "counterculture" she described it as a prolonged panty raid. The righteous indignation, against virtually everything, being wailed from cabaret to cabaret was to her nothing but a stylish temper tantrum.

She was no longer in it for the ideals. She was in it for the business.

"Days like this," groaned Paul Hogan, "make me wish I'd never started the whole thing."

"Sure is some monster you created," said Gloria. "Lucky us."

Cliff had been Paul Hogan's big break. Second-raters, second-stringers had been his usual fare. His people were usually the opening acts for the real stars and not until Cliff came along had he had anything close to a headliner.

He had caught Cliff's act in Philadelphia even before JFK became president. While Kennedy was just beginning to enchant the nation as a candidate of vigor, Cliff was doing garden variety stand-up at a place in Jenkintown called the Blue Note, one of a thousand Greenwich Village-coffeehouse wannabes that had sprung up coast to coast in reflection of the action emanating from downtown Manhattan.

Cliff's gags were mostly all right. The college crowd was appreciative of his efforts, even though the kids talked through most of the performance. Toward the end, though, Cliff tossed in some Kennedy - and the response was electric! Paul Hogan, who'd been scouting from city to city, sat there stunned. The take-off was perfect. Backstage, Paul urged Cliff to enlarge the Kennedy, but Cliff resisted. The other material was more important to him.

Important but not triumphant, said Paul. The Kennedy is a winner. The Kennedy is your ticket. Do you really want to spend the rest of your life in back street dives? Thus, his eyes open to the obvious, but demurring all the way, Cliff gradually switched his act to Kennedy in total, and a headliner was born. Paul booked him into the Café Muse to expose him to the uptown suites. Joe Franklin and Ed Sullivan and Jack Paar and Steve Allen came calling. No more dives.

"We're using the kid," said Paul. "We won't even stop him for a bomb."

"There's no fucking bomb," said Gloria, "and quit griping."

"The guy has no life. He can't even walk down the street without being mobbed."

"You were happier when you were both down and out?"

119

Paul gave this some thought. "Maybe I was. Maybe I was."

"Hey," Gloria snapped, "you want your boy back, you'll get your boy back. Just give it time. This is America, remember? We're a nation of fads. We play with something and then we tire of it and play with something else. Think of him as today's hula hoop, like Lenny said - here today, gone tomorrow. If it's failure and obscurity you want, don't fret. It'll come. Just wait till Kennedy gets us into a recession or a war or something - and then try to book Cliff Harris!"

Nate Beloff agreed, to an extent. Nate as a run-of-the-mill club owner had already had his own share of obscurity and never imagined himself the proprietor of America's number one attraction. These were boom times for him. But there had been a certain charm to the sleepier days when his club had been half-empty but a tryout haven to luckless but sincere artists who gave their hearts away up there on stage. Nate missed those days. He did not miss them enough to even think of trading them in for what he had today. Today he had the dream of every club owner, the biggest hit in town. Even at this moment the crowds were still surging to get in. There were pockets of rioting.

There was a bomb threat. The cops were all over the place. Plainly, he held title to a blessing and a curse. He often wondered which would prevail.

Chapter 17

Somewhere in the middle of Cliff Harris' performance - Ben Jaffa was gone. Louise Carmen turned around, and there he wasn't. The place was so dark and so crowded and so taken in by Cliff that in a blink she had lost him; and only moments before they had been exchanging smiles and holding hands. He'd been distracted and edgy, but was he crazy, too? She knew exactly where he was.

Ben had decided that this was the moment to confront Jimmy Bleeds with ultimatums. The flame of indignation singed him when he saw in Cliff's performance (lackluster as it was for the time being) the true value, and the rewards, of a work of love. Meanwhile Ben's own work of love belonged to another man, Jimmy Bleeds.

The injustice was too much for Ben. In previous encounters Jimmy Bleeds had snickered that there was nothing personal in the theft. To Ben it was nothing but personal, since his oppressor came from a tribe that had tormented his people in a past not so long ago.

The Ukranians often outdid the Nazis. Given the nod by the Gestapo, Ukrainian gangs rounded up Ben's people by the thousands, herded them into the woods and let loose a campaign of unspeakable rape and slaughter. Ben had thought he was finished with this. That was the past, and were he to keep remembering there'd be no end to the list of evildoers, beginning with the Germans, followed by the

French, the Poles, the Slavs, the Croats, the Hungarians, the Czechs, the Romanians, the Russians - they were all "the worst" in the words of any survivor.

These were not grudges you brought along as you passed the Statue of Liberty. You forgot, or you tried to forget. You were finally in America where you let bygones be bygones, set aside old hatreds, shed ancient animosities, and acquired new ones, new prejudices, but American ones.

But Jimmy Bleeds brought it all back to Ben. Each man has his own Hitler and Jimmy Bleeds was Ben's Hitler of the moment.

The raw theft of his work was an indication to Ben that the fight was not over, would never be over; the Roundup of Paris would thrive and survive and fester in different places, under different names - everything would change but the torment itself.

Each generation brought forth a new villain. Ben knew the history and he knew the Biblical prophecy that there'd be no end to Pharaoh and he was determined to let others turn the other cheek. He'd pass over the 2,000 years of Jewish passivity and hark back to Joshua and King David. That's why he turned to martial arts and joined the Israeli Army at the age of 18. As an American volunteer, he served mostly in the frontier with Jordan and after seven months, after being slightly wounded in a flare-up along the border, he went back home to Cincinnati and later resumed his studies at Ohio State. He loved Israel as a child loves a mother, but he loved America as a husband loves a wife.

The door to Jimmy Bleeds' Improv City was locked, but Ben heard the dog barking, so he knew Jimmy Bleeds had to be inside. Ben kept knocking on the door to no avail and so finally he found an opening in a back window and let himself in.

The dog lunged at Ben and stopped dead in its tracks and folded submissively when Ben snapped to the combat-ready Krav Maga forward-outlet stance. That was the easy part. Next came Jimmy Bleeds who, it turned out, had been screwing some chick on the cot next to his desk and was not at all horrified to find Ben intruding.

"Can you wait till I'm done?" he said plaintively.

Some of the fight went out of Ben to find the man so vulnerable. He had expected an immediate confrontation. Not this. Ben recognized the girl as a waitress in the Fast Tempo on Grove Street. She was black and beautiful and after escorting her out, Jimmy Bleeds said, "Just doing my part for racial harmony. Isn't that what you kids are after?"

"You're a regular Freedom Rider."

"I like that," said Jimmy Bleeds lighting up a cigarette Humphrey Bogart style. Ben was beginning to feel very *film noir.* The scar running down Jimmy Bleeds' left cheek only added to the sense of *déjà vu.* This scene, Ben thought, had been played before.

Everything about the interior of Improv City bespoke an era of the 30s, 40s and early 50s. Photos, mementos and letters of friendship from Babe Ruth, Joe Louis, Rocky Marciano, Rocky Graziano, Ben Hecht, Jayne Mansfield, Jimmy Cannon, Ernest Hemingway, Gorgeous George, Edward G. Robinson, lined the walls.

Jimmy Bleeds caught Ben staring at it all awestruck.

"Yeah, those were the days," he said wistfully. "You'll never know what the Village was really like."

Then he added: "You kids are too late. *Everything has already happened.*"

Jimmy Bleeds was cunning enough to know that Ben had come with the fire of a battler. But Jimmy Bleeds knew the art of softening his opponent. He'd been a boxer himself and knew the value of light jabs before the big sucker punch.

Yes, he said, falling into a trance of nostalgia, Dorothy Parker had read her withering poetry right here in the spot where Ben was standing. Marlene Dietrich had played strip poker with Ernest fucking Hemingway right there at that table in front of the stage while Rudy Vallee was belting out "My Time Is Your Time."

Barrymore, he forgot which one, once got so stinking drunk he nearly wrecked the joint.

All of it happened here, in this very dive, back when there were real people. Like Clark Gable.

"Nobody's real anymore," Jimmy Bleeds said mournfully. "I mean authentic is what I mean."

Humorists? Mort Sahl couldn't hold a candle to Ring Lardner.

You want sassy? Lenny Bruce couldn't lay a glove on Dorothy Parker, with all his *Seven Dirty Words*.

"Mickey and Whitey still come around, and they're real, they're authentic. But I had *Babe Ruth* here once. Babe Ruth and Lou Gehrig, bless his soul. They were here with their wives and you know it's their wives who hated each other and caused that split between Ruth and Gehrig. But that one night they were all here to celebrate Mrs. Ruth's birthday and everybody got along. They behaved." Jimmy Bleeds stared off in the distance and then laughed. "Nobody else did, though. Not in those days."

Ben had come to talk about this day, this very day that had Jimmy Bleeds' name up on the marquee proclaiming himself the author of Ben's Nobel Prize routine. But Ben was trapped. He was a sucker for nostalgia. Actually he was a soft touch for Americana. He hungered for the hometown he never had and nostalgia was news from an America he knew not but flourished in his heart. Nostalgia was his hometown.

Today, Jimmy Bleeds declared, it's all Holden Caulfield.

"That's what started it, ten years ago. Everybody wanted to be cynical and disenchanted, just like their hero. Beats, beatniks, they all flow back to the same source. The Bohemians - that's where I came in - and they were really fucking Bohemian. You talk about your starving writers and artists. I had a soup kitchen out back, right by the window where you slipped in. Thomas Wolfe? Middle of the night, after Johnny Ray cried his lungs out there on stage, I had to pick him up off the ground at Bleecker and MacDougal. Yeah, Thomas Wolfe. He was sleeping on the corner, dead of winter."

The point of it all being that those were real people. Ben, like the rest of his generation, was not real.

Not authentic.

Ironically, this was a generation of phonies - precisely what Caulfield had been pissing and moaning about.

"I mean so what!" Jimmy Bleeds said, finally striking a confrontational pose, eyes bulging and his flesh lathering up in red sweat. "So fucking what? You wrote a skit. All right. Fine. My hat's off to you. So me, I cribbed. All right? Let's be frank. Yeah, I cribbed. If I cribbed off Hemingway, say, would he give a shit? That's what I mean by authentic. Hey listen, Ben. I'm talking to you like a father. I mean I haven't been showing you around and telling you things for nothing. I'm trying to teach you to be *big*. Be big, Mr. Jaffa. Cross that line. As you can see, I am not the craven sonofabitch you think I am. Let me tell you something. People are complex. Good people do bad things. Bad people do good things. Goes on all the time. Plagiarism's nothing new.

"Hemingway plagiarized. Yeah, he did, when he was in high school or something. But he did. Every fucking body plagiarizes Mozart, just like today everybody's plagiarizing Zimmerman across the street. You know who Zimmerman is, don't you? Bob Dylan. Shit, he plagiarized his *name* from Dylan Thomas."

Ben was speechless. He had never heard a case for theft made so eloquently.

"Listen," Jimmy Bleeds continued, "everything's a copy of something. No such thing as *original*. You know your Bible. Nothing's new under the sun. I don't look the type. I know, but I read, had to keep up with the people I dealt with, and let me tell you, you read Salinger and you might as well be reading Mark Twain."

Ben tried to get things back to this time and this place. "You're changing the subject," he said.

"Hey, I thought this is the subject, about me copying you!"

"That wasn't *copying*, Jimmy. That wasn't *homage*! That was stealing. You put your name on my skit."

Ben stood his ground and clenched his fists as Jimmy Bleeds began to puff up his chest to diminish the adversary. They were in close quarters, Jimmy Bleeds beginning a cornering technique. This could turn into a cockfight and Ben was preparing himself. He'd been made soft by the man's trip down memory lane and rendered gullible by the man's literary sleight of hand. He'd have to dig deep inside himself to rekindle the rage. "Yeah," said Jimmy Bleeds, "I stole. I got carried away. So? What are your options? You gonna kill me?"

"The thought did cross my mind," Ben said fearlessly.

Ben expected something tough in return. Instead, Jimmy Bleeds turned to mush.

"I'm dying," he said in a whimpering tone.

Ben said, "We're all dying."

"You don't understand."

What Ben didn't understand was that Jimmy Bleeds was dying from a disease Jimmy Bleeds didn't want to mention.

Ben said he was sorry, but what did that have to do with anything?

"Ben, you're young. There'll be other skits. You'll write entire plays. Who knows what's ahead for you. Me? Where am I going? That's what we have to consider. All my life I've wanted to do something *authentic*. You know, like that crowd that used to come in here."

"You wanted to be big."

"Now we're talking. Yeah, big. I wanted to be big. Now does it all make sense?"

The man was making an emotional appeal. Ben - hating himself for it - was touched.

"You wrote a wonderful skit, young man," Jimmy Bleeds continued. "I saw something there that I could never do and to be honest I figured you'd forget about it, you just being a doorman across the street. No offense intended, but you're not one of the big boys around here, you're a fucking doorman!"

Ben quickened. He was being played for a sucker. "Wait a fucking minute..."

So that was the game, Jimmy Bleeds doing good cop-bad cop all in one. Switching back and forth.

Ben was catching on.

"You're a fucking nobody, Ben. I've seen your kind come and go. Like tumbleweeds. Get me?"

Jimmy Bleeds went on to say that doormen at the Bitter End had a certain mystique about them, a magnetism, a gallantry that helped draw the crowds, by all means the women, never mind the headliner. Fred Weintraub sure knew his business. No other coffeehouse had quite the same magic out front. A doorman at the Bitter End was a star in his own right. Ben Jaffa was true to the format. But - they came and they went. As would Ben.

"Here's the deal," said Jimmy Bleeds. "You go back to where you came from..."

Ben did not care for the insinuation. "What's that supposed to mean?"

"Nothing except that we all come from someplace. So you go back, but go back knowing that you made a sick old man happy. Me, I get some appreciation, finally. Listen, you want money? I'll pay. That square us?"

Ben said all he wanted was his *name*.

"All right. Suppose this. Equal billing. Co-authorship."

This was no sucker punch, but a pretty solid round-house. Ben was stunned by the blow.

"Did you hear what I said? You and me both. What do you say?"

"Why should I share my name with you?"

Jimmy Bleeds turned livid. "Jesus Christ, man. I'm doing you a favor!"

"You're doing *me* a favor?"

"Well what the fuck have you got now? Nothing. So I'm giving you something. Equal billing."

"That's your offer."

"I think I'm being very generous. So it's a deal?"

Ben had some fast thinking to do. "Why co-authorship when I created the whole thing myself?"

"NOBODY BUT GOD CREATES EVERYTHING BY HIMSELF."

There was no getting around that reasoning.

"Think it over," Jimmy Bleeds said. "You came in here all pissed off. You're leaving a winner."

Ben had expected the confrontation to lead to fisticuffs. That's what he had wanted. A quick knockout punch, something decisive - and then declare himself a winner. Instead he had allowed himself to be out-talked and outfoxed. He had let it fizzle and he'd leave once again with nothing decisive to show for all his righteous indignation.

The offer was too good to turn down, and too lousy to take up.

That's where things stood. No, Jimmy Bleeds was the winner.

They seem to always win, Ben was thinking as he slammed the door behind him and rushed back to the Café Muse.

Chapter 18

Ben got back just in time for the intermission. Louise asked no questions and Ben gave no answers. Louise was simply thrilled to see him - alive. "I love you so much," she whispered as Ben settled in beside her. She is so young, Ben thought happily. She is so young, Ben though sadly.

Though the table was thick with people, it was dark enough for Louise to make her special request. "You know what to do," she said, slipping him those big playful brown eyes. Yes he did. He knew exactly what to do. He swept his right arm inside the back of here sweater, reached around her braless contours, found her nipples hard and ready and began to fool with them as she braced herself for an oncoming orgasm. Her breathing came fast and in gusts of pleasure. "Oh Ben," she kept sighing as an incantation as she squirmed in her seat and her eyes began to moisten.

"You've got magical hands," she said. Then: "Yes - go there. Don't be afraid."

She could not be heard as the intermission had turned into a free-for-all jam session. She could not be seen, either, for the lights were still dim. No one saw the heated action at Louise's table except for Howie, who, as usual, had been standing in the lobby for a better view of things. Richie was at some other table with some other friends. Ben and Louise...Howie thought it might earn him some points if he whispered something in Richie's ear.

Intermissions were something new for Cliff Harris, who was now alone in his dressing room recovering from the first segment of his show and preparing himself for the next. After the album came out audiences demanded some of that electrifying extra material, so Cliff was persuaded to lengthen his performances, but with a break.

Neither Gloria MacKenzie, or Paul Hogan, or Nate Beloff dared enter his dressing room when he took that break. He was "in character" and not to be disturbed. This afternoon he needed that privacy to restrain his anger against the lady who kept coughing in the second row, interrupting his timing throughout. For an instant he considered giving her a heckler's *shpritz*. But that wouldn't be Kennedy.

But it was a commentary on the kind of people you got for a matinee. *Tourists! Stay home!* He had also heard the phone ring in the back, and that too had disrupted him. Of course he did not know what the phone call was all about, was not about to ask, was not about to be told.

For the blood, guts and glory he'd need to face the people again he had Beethoven's Ninth blaring from the record player. He struck a conductor's pose and thus led the orchestra, arms violently criss-crossing the air. There he stood in reverential silence to pay homage to the majesty of such talent, such sublime genius. Then he wept. He wept for Beethoven - the greatest of all composers - deaf. Again the work of the celestial prankster.

He was out of character and would have to work his way back in. An emotionally-crazed weeping Kennedy would not do.

* * *

For Louise Carmen this was the best of times. She had Ben by her side and Richie hooked and she was in a crowded café among the savant, the artist, the avant-garde, which put her right there with the Algonquin and the Deux Magots of yesteryears. She was smoking her Gaulois and feeling very smart, chic and intellectual. She was young, the youngest of the Highlight Singers who were gathered at another table nearby, but she was part of the scene, in fact the prettiest part, issuing from the stage. She belonged to a set of rebels who were going to *change things*, and just being here among them stimulated her.

She knew Richie was sulking, but he'd get over it as he always did. Anyway, this was her moment and no lover's spat was worthy of concern. She felt herself blessed to be part of a bold, new beginning. She felt blessed to be at the center of her ardent generation. This was her place, her time.

Virtually all of Greenwich Village's headliners and notables had volunteered their services to support the Freedom Riders and were here doing an impromptu benefit during Cliff Harris' intermission. The jam to support activists who had taken to the road for civil rights included Bob Dylan, Peter, Paul and Mary, Joan Baez, Judy Collins or their look-alikes and now that was Tiny Tim up there with his ukulele.

Spirits were high even though the cause was about such things as freedom and liberation, freedom from oppression and the liberation of blacks. From the stage and from the spectators, in song and in speech, the call went out for brotherhood. There was talk against the Establishment and the war machine being devised by McNamara and Rusk for Vietnam. There were prophesies of war and complaints against the fuzz who were harassing such groups as homosexuals and lesbians and such individuals as Lenny Bruce. A euphony of guitars, banjos and bongo drums kept it all in rhythm.

Even the squares applauded and snapped their fingers even though back home they probably disapproved of the causes they were sanctioning in the heat of the moment. The hat passed around for the Freedom Riders. The locals dropped in quarters; the tourists deposited dollar bills.

"This is so terrific," said Louise, beaming and snuggling up to Ben, who was enjoying it all with a sense of bemusement. He did not understand. He tried to understand but he did not understand. So much of it eluded him.

"I guess," he said, shrugging and offering a weak smile.

"You guess?"

"I guess."

"Don't you feel it?"

"I feel it," he shrugged.

"Oh, Ben."

"What can I say?"

"That you feel the pulse!"

"I feel the pulse," he said.

"Oh, Ben. Ben, Ben, Ben." So detached, thought Louise. But then again, that was part of his charm.

Louise took Ben's disconnectedness as Ben's just being *cool*. That was some of it, but most of it was puzzlement as to what the griping was all about. So much griping, yes, in very nice language, in very pretty ballads, but about what? The Government? The Establishment? The fuzz?

Really. Well, went Ben's reasoning, if you really think this country is bad, try Germany and France and in fact all of Europe 20 years ago. Now that was *bad*. That was Government, that was Establishment, that was fuzz all right.

This? This is peanuts.

This is a picnic. America is a picnic and it is only the Americans who do not know it.

"Aren't you glad to be with me?" Louise pouted, thinking there was some deficiency in her.

Ben kissed her gently on the cheek. He'd never reveal his true thoughts to her. She would not understand.

He did not want her to understand.

"I want you to be happy, Ben," she whispered.

"I am."

"I mean, I always want you to associate happiness with me. I mean now and forever."

Always picture me, she went on to say, when you think of happiness. "Even when we're apart and you're long gone."

She spoke as someone who knew this moment would never come round again. Things were just too good. She was too happy. Something was bound to happen if not now, then later, if not her, then to Richie, and if not Richie, then to Ben. But something was bound to happen to change everything. She faced Ben with a no-nonsense expression, as if to say there is a woman inside this child. "Always picture me as I am tonight, Ben. Picture us as we were tonight." She kissed him hard on the lips. "Keep the moments as souvenirs."

That he would do.

If America was a picnic, Louise Carmen was the feast. Besides zestful and warmhearted, the word for her was wholesome and it was that virtue that made her, and the rest of the Highlight Singers, the toast of both Americas, the hip and the square. The Highlights were not raunchy, but they were naughty. They were the debutantes, the coeds, the cheerleaders who were no threat to custom but were rather the safe and delightful flirts and prick-teasers - as in their suggestive rendition of "All I Want for Christmas..."

But squeaky-clean Louise Carmen had brought two dozen Trojans with her from Wheeling and had Ben use half of them in quick order beginning in the back room of Asti's restaurant on East 12th where the waiters and waitresses sang for the customers. She had unzipped him under the tablecloths at the Duplex Club on Grove Street and at Patrissy's Italian restaurant on Kenmore while Frank Sinatra was dining several tables away. She thrilled him minute to minute.

Yet - there was something so undeniably tragic about her. Her ravenous appetite for life revealed a dimension beyond simple jubilation. Something else was at work, most apparent in her petitions to be loved - to be loved not completely but "just a little bit," which suggested a fear of being consumed by permanence when it was all so transitory. She'd fall into no such trap as to give or be given anything in its entirety - anything or anybody.

She lived for the moments, almost literally so, as hours, days, weeks, months, years were all too vague and too far ahead to be worthy of consideration.

Day after day, night after night that is, she *schlepped* Richie and Ben from one bistro to another not so much for the pleasures of Streisand and Baez and Dylan and all the rest but for the fear of missing out on something, something that would be here only once and then be gone forever.

She was squirreling away memories; saving them up for a lifetime of rainy days. In that headlong rush from escapade to escapade she had made this past summer an extraordinary caper, and not just for herself but for everyone around her. They all shared her contagious excitements.

Let's go here, let's go there, let's do this, let's do that - seldom a moment to catch your breath. She even managed to persuade Ben to take in the transvestites at the Crazy Horse, Ben did not care for that kind of thing, and actually neither did she - but it was something new and something to do, and anything to do was not to be missed.

That time with Ben at the Metropole up Broadway when she got up from the table and did an impromptu strip to the beat of Gene Krupa, now that was something new - and she even did it better than the pros. "I can do better than that," she said to Ben, and did. She took it *all* off and the place went nuts.

Ben had never been so turned on.

The time some weeks back up Fifth Avenue when she darted out in traffic to play chicken, that was also new - and terrifying. "So spank me for being a bad girl," she later said seductively to Ben. He spanked her all right and wondered, what's this all about, this living life on a dare?

She thanked him for saving her but he had not really saved her, she said. People have got it all wrong when they say so and so saved another person's life. There is no such thing. All you did was postpone that person's death. If you really *saved* a person's life that meant you saved that person's life forever. But nobody lives forever. All you did was postpone the inevitable.

Ben guessed that that was the hillbilly in her doing such talk. Miners were saved - but they still died, some the very next day. Did she believe in God? In a creator, yes, in God, no. Then, said Ben, you do not believe in an afterlife, either.

She laughed. Do you? she asked. Do you really? Do you really believe there is such a thing?

Yes.

Oh, Ben, you can be so *Jewish*.

You *goyim* believe it, too.

Not this *goy*, she said. Not this *shiksa*. Come on Ben, there's Santa Claus, the tooth fairy, and then there's your afterlife. Like we're all going to end up in some paradise, right? Oh please, Ben, not from you. You've been to hell and you believe in heaven? Poor Ben. Poor everybody. I guess people need *something* to believe in, something other than the moments that keep ticking by. Me, I believe in the moments. The moments, Ben, that's God.

Moments, that was God. Memories, those were the angels.

That was months ago, in the heart of summer when that discussion took place and it was never touched upon again. Too serious; it had all been too serious and she regretted delving so into her true self, revealing herself so. That would never happen again. Ben had sucked her in. Oh she'd talk philosophy all day, so long as it was abstract. This had been too personal.

Now, in the warmth of the Café Muse, Cliff's intermission offering up a kaleidoscope of talent and Louise thrilling to each *moment*, the moments she veritably worshiped, she offered her lips to Ben as a sign of explicit gladness, gladness for Ben being Ben, gladness for being here with him and with all the rest of the people, Greenwich Village people, who were so dear to her, gladness for being here to share the high point of the season - though that could be said for any day so far as Louise was concerned.

Ben kissed her quivering lips, but it was not a romantic kiss.

There was something in his kiss that suggested farewell, and in fact Ben had his own vision of things to come and his vision differed from Louise's only in details. She smiled and squeezed his hand. She would not understand this either, his duty to join the Navy. This jamming was all *against* the devotion to arms.

Just now, in fact, Bob Dylan's emotionally-charged anti-war anthem rang out from the stage. *Now ye masters of war... you who build the big guns... I just want you to know you're playing with my world... You put a gun in my hand... You hide your face from my eyes... You turn and run farther when the fast bullets fly...*

This brought them to their feet cheering, hand clapping and finger snapping, except for Louise, who sat there sobered by the moralizing power of those words. Such prophetic insights seemed to be aimed directly at her, her and her two lovers. Ben was going, of that she had no doubt, and as for Richie, had he really been deferred as he kept insisting when she asked him about those unopened envelopes stamped Selective Service? She chose to believe that he was 4-F only to keep the high-spirited instants alive, but she suspected that a terrible truth awaited her. She was about to lose the two most important men in her life. This she saw too clearly.

She'd never show it, never let it surface to her sparkling eyes and through her bubbly ways, but she had begun to grieve for the loss of *everything*. Yes, she too was leaving, but not forever, like possibly the rest of everybody and everything.

She was coming back from Wheeling in but a matter of weeks and she so wanted things to be the same, Richie where he belonged, waiting tables at the Village Gate as Miriam Makeba, Odetta and Richard Pryor performed on stage; Ben where he belonged, so princely at the door of the Bitter End, Cliff where he belonged, regaling them at the Café Muse; all of it, the bustle of the streets come evening, the excitement in the cabarets, the stimulating get-togethers at the Hip Bagel and McSorely's, the chess and cider parties at the Café Feenjon as Mailer and Capote and Styron and Jones engaged in intellectual duels, every moment a new experience - all of this she imagined as a portrait frozen in time.

Or rather, she feared that it might tarnish in a snap. In a recurring nightmare she saw herself returning to a Greenwich Village that was closed, desolate and deserted, shut down like a play that had finished its run.

If not this time, then another time. There was nothing quite like that hollow feeling of good things coming to an end.

If only, she was now thinking, she and she alone could come and go as she pleased while everyone else stayed put!

People had no right to come and go as they pleased - those people and places she loved.

If things had to change and people had to go, at the least, she hoped - let it all start over again next summer. Was that too much to ask? Let things be the same, was all she asked. She did not even want things to be better, just the same, the same as they had been in the spring and autumn of 1963.

She was at fault for a fraction of the break-up; this much she knew or rather imagined. Partly from pique and partly from innocence she thought Ben and perhaps Richie, yes Richie, had the military on their minds solely to escape the entrapment of the nest. (Richie liked to kid how dashing he'd look in uniform.) That's why men ran off to war, she thought - to escape their women. Neither blood feuds, territorial imperatives, religious animosity, nationalistic fervor, regional disputes, nor ethnic grudges adequately explained the cause for war.

No, it was all about women.

But going off to Wheeling was her doing, not Richie's or Ben's or anybody's. Her career was on the move and she had to hearken to its demands and anyway, she needed the pause to sort out her love live and take a breather from the potency of Village life.

She needed to get away from Greenwich Village (if only for a spell) as she had once needed to get away from Wheeling. After so many nights in the confined company of poets, writers, artists, actors, social and political activists, she yearned for the open road and wide open spaces and the vitality of people who worked with their hands and were concerned more with their crops than their careers - or the Government or the Establishment.

So much strife - everyone so fervent, everyone out to save themselves or the nation or even the entire world - got to be a burden for a simple girl. She was, after all, a country girl and once in a while she needed to feel the earth and regain her sense of simplicity.

But she'd be back, and if only the same could be said for the rest of them.

After the Dylan number, Miriam Makeba took the stage. Stunningly beautiful black dancers twirled around her to the rhythm of African bongos. The sensuality of the music and dancing sent the room vibrating, every man and woman in tempo and utterly adrift from the world outside.

Even the squares had the beat. Even the straights from Cleveland lost their inhibitions.

More guards were posted by the doors to prevent the envious overflows from storming in.

The back doors had to be bolted in violation of fire ordinances. New York's police commissioner Michael J. ("Skull") Murphy had personally visited the Café Muse and warned Gloria MacKenzie about such breaches, but Gloria was Gloria. The show was the thing.

Sirens wailed outside but no one heard them inside.

The improvisational interlude ended with Makeba. The stage was empty and there was silence in anticipation of Cliff Harris' return. There was some whispering that James Dean was in attendance, along with Marilyn Monroe. Both were dead. Monroe had died the year before and Dean was dead 10 years.

But the people yearned for idols and thus look-alikes abounded throughout America as did conspiracy theories.

James Dean, it was said, had not been killed in an automobile accident. He was hiding from his worshipful fans.

Ironically, in death he was worshiped as even more godlike and in his memory young men combed their hair high, slouched, mumbled and scowled, sometimes attracting women who resembled Marilyn Monroe, another figure of worship. Platinum blondes prevailed.

In any case, heroes real or emulated, dead or alive, were the objects of intense worship in America. America gloried in its heroes perhaps because they were heroes or merely distractions against Khrushchev's threats to bomb the nation to smithereens and Kennedy's call to "pay any price, bear any burden, meet any hardship, support any friend."

That was some task for a people that liked to frolic and raised its movie stars, not its generals or politicians, to the rank of royalty. Americans were prepared to be reinvigorated but were skeptical about the burdens and the price.

Soon another rumor spread throughout the room that the Rat Pack headed by Frank Sinatra had left Jilly's on 48th and was headed down here with Judy Garland to attend the latter part of Cliff Harris' performance.

The stage lights flickered and "Hail to the Chief" came booming from the loudspeakers.

Cliff Harris, a.k.a., John Kennedy, was back.

"Jackie says hello...from Paris," Cliff began.

The people whistled, cheered and applauded and held on for more.

"Let me say this about that. Yes it's true that I-ya made Bobby my attorney general. It's also true that Bobby is my-ah younger brother. But let me assure you that the one had nothing to do with the oth-ah. It was between Bobby or-ah Baby John-John."

They laughed and he was in the groove. "People ausk-me about the Pope. If I-ya take orders from him. I take orders from nobody. I am the-ah president of the United

States. No one tells me what to do. Not Congress, not the Supreme Court, not...Be right with you Jackie."

These were not jokes really, but mere harmless mischief being directed at a playful president by a playful America, which could never imagine itself enjoying such mirth at the expense of the august and elderly Eisenhower.

This, then, was a release from the do-nothing bondage of the 1950s. The nation was delighting in its newly-found irreverence. Taking pot shots at national leaders, including presidents, was nothing new, except that with Kennedy the humor was for, not against.

What if Lyndon Johnson (now merely vice-president) had defeated Kennedy in the 1960 Democratic National Convention? No one could imagine such merriment being played on the gloomy heavy-footed Texan. Or what if Richard Nixon had defeated Kennedy in the general election that followed?

Nixon?

But none of those ifs had transpired and the nation felt blessed - or rather part of the population appreciated the outcome.

(Considering how soundly Kennedy had whipped Nixon in the TV debates, and how Kennedy seemingly represented light over Nixon's darkness, it was revealing that in the end Kennedy had defeated Nixon by fewer than 120,000 popular votes. All along there had been another America as well.)

"Oh that!" said Cliff, rolling along. "I'm glad you ausked that question. No, Jackie was not jealous when Marilyn Monroe sang Happy Birthday for me in Madison Square Garden, and I'ya certainly was not offended by the-ah sultry approach to the lyrics sung by-ah Miss Monroe. She may have been a-ah blonde bombshell to the-ah rest of Americker. To me she was a-ah registered Democrat."

Gazing across the darkened room - dark save for the spotlight on him on stage and the candles flickering on what seemed like a thousand tiny checkerbox tables - seeing these happy, laughing faces, it struck Cliff how young everybody was. Or seemed to be. There were no old people here at the Café Muse today or any other day. There were no old people in America period. Not with Kennedy in office.

"Yes, Jackie," Cliff said moving swiftly from *shpritz* to *shpritz*. "I know it's time for my-ah French lesson. Yes, Jackie, I know it was wrong of Caroline to sit on Mr. DeGaulle's lap. So here goes. I-ah parley Frauncey inky-ah dinky-ah parley vous."

That had been big in the album and was big again today. Impeccable timing, this was, matched only by the precise exultation wafting back in return, precise in that each punch line was met with appropriate response at the exact instant it was called for, so that it had the effect of a piano virtuoso in sweet harmony with the orchestra, the give and take just right, and entire room, an entire universe in cadence and in harmony.

Chapter 19

News drifted slowly through the arteries of Greenwich Village, so while much of the nation already had word, here in Greenwich Village, an exile of artistic indifference to the world at large, a place that quickened to the esthetic but slumbered through headline events, the word was just beginning to arrive but making its way gradually and skeptically from doorpost to doorpost.

During the intermission Patrolman Ornstein - who'd had his premonitions (confirmed) from and incident earlier in the day - approached Howie, who was smoking outside, and asked if he knew. Howie said yes, he knew, there were enough cops mounted and on foot patrol to tell him. So had he told the people inside?

"If anybody should be the first to know," said Ornstein, "it's the people inside the Café Muse."

Howie said yes, he had passed the news along to Gloria and to Nate and even personally to Cliff backstage.

"You're sure," said Ornstein.

"Hey, I'm sure," said Howie. "I've taken care of everything."

"So how come the show is still going on?"

"Beats me," said Howie.

Ornstein walked away and kept shaking his head muttering, "That's show biz, I guess."

Howie of course, had not taken care of everything or anything. Howie decided to keep the news to himself out of a sense of loyalty and spite. There was nothing to be gained from stopping the show and everything to be gained to be in the possession of such power, the power of information. Information given, information withheld. Same thing. Stuart Ball, the lethargic doorman of the Café Muse, recently hired and soon to be fired, was busy enough with the overflow multitudes and so asked Howie to step inside and pass the word. All Howie did was step inside to join the fun. Howie did not much care for Kennedy and anyway it was probably just a rumor. He did hop around 50 tables in the dark and walked over to Richie to tell him about all the fuzz outside and about the word that was filtering through the grapevine. Richie chuckled and agreed. Probably just a rumor. "Sounds just like something Lenny would cook up just to needle Cliff," said Richie, gesturing to the table where Lenny was sitting with his entourage.

But John Kennedy was dead.

He was shot at 1:30 p.m. New York time and died instantly. Since a wider conspiracy was suspected, his death was not made official until 2 p.m. to secure Secret Service protection for Vice President Lyndon Johnson from the moment he assumed the presidency.

Minutes after the shots were fired from the Texas School Book Depository the news spread domestically and abroad as from blood weeping to the heavens. Reactions varied from grief to disbelief and if there was ever a time when the world stopped, this was the moment.

Radio and television were the first messengers of evil tidings but much of the nationwide information came in secondhand, from friends, neighbors, pedestrians, motorists and co-workers. Because of the hour, most people were at work or in school and because the tragedy was so great and so incomprehensible - who could imagine the sudden fall of a knight so comely, vigorous and mighty? - many doubted, or wanted to doubt, the veracity of the initial reports.

Was it a mistake? A hoax? Teachers were reluctant to pass the word to students - this was the day of Prom Night among numerous school districts that were celebrating mid-year graduation - and some kids heard nothing until they left class.

A good number of men and women at work were kept in the dark until much later in the day, and throughout, until the president was pronounced dead, and even past the time, people still clung to the hope that the president would recover. He had to recover. He was the president, more powerful than all of us, and he was Kennedy, John Kennedy, Jack.

On orders from Commissioner Murphy, New York police were dispatched to protect Mayor Robert F. Wagner and other city dignitaries. A special alarm went out to the Sixth District for reinforcements. Police officers were alerted to secure a detail for the Café Muse, in particular around the deceased president's double, Cliff Harris. Conspiracy was in the air.

If the president was vulnerable, who wasn't?

Chapter 20

Cliff had them roaring with his spoof of a touch football game on Martha's Vineyard, Jack explaining to a childishly intractable Bobby why he, Jack, should be the quarterback. "I am the-ah quarterback because I am the-ah president. That's why." Pause. "Now stop crying Bobby, or I won't let you play attorney general any-moe-ah."

He was leading up to *sick shtick* but meanwhile that one had them in stitches.

But at Louise's table there was awkwardness. Richie Bell had decided to pull up a chair between Ben and Louise and he was his old carefree self. "Are we friends?" said Louise, testing.

Richie chuckled and said of course, and meant it; he'd come to accept Wheeling as just another fling of hers that he'd have to live through before he settled her down. Ben was another story, in fact a story related to him by Howie, about what had been going on between Ben and Louise over and under the table, and this was practically unforgivable as this had been the deal: no fooling around with her if the other guy was in the same room.

"Enjoying yourself?" asked Ben.

Richie did not respond.

"Ben asked you something," said Louise.

"I heard," Richie said flatly. "I'm trying to listen to the show."

"Oh," said Louise. "Like you never heard this before."

"Only in the living room."

"He doesn't want to talk, Louise," said Ben. "Leave the guy alone."

"He doesn't want to talk to *you*. Richie, please, let's have peace."

"I hear Ben's already had some."

Louise took it well and merely smiled. Louise did not mind a portion of jealousy here and there from her two great loves. She would mind it if it went too far. Their friendship toward each other was precious to her and she'd be shattered to think of herself as the cause of a split. This, this was just a spat. They'd get over it; Richie never kept a grudge. Ben, however, did not take it well.

So now it was out and Ben even knew the rat. Always Howie. Only this time Richie had not told him to shut up. Ben was sorry. Richie was his one true friend. Ben would have to find ways to make amends, most likely by just letting it drop. This much he had to consider, that in the end it would be Richie and Louise, not Ben and Louise, yes Richie and Louise, so perhaps the time was approaching to make the announcement. No, not now. Always not now.

Besides, it was Richie who had news - news that he was not prepared to reveal.

The cops had spooked him back there on Sullivan Street and he knew they'd be back. He was not afraid, he had nothing to hide, maybe, but he did not like complications. So there was one answer and it had come in one of those letters from the Selective Service Board. Before leaving the apartment he decided to open one of the envelopes and sure enough UNCLE SAM still wanted him, in December. That was next month.

Despite his poor health, he had undergone the required physical at the Selective Service office in Hartford right after high school and he was declared 1-A, which was a laugh, but a secret he kept from everyone, including Sally Caruthers, the-girl-back-home. She'd make a scene and would not   recognize the hilarity of the situation. Richie Bell a soldier?

Only his parents knew. His dad had been a hero in WWII and thought it only proper that his son do his duty.

Anyhow, forgetting the Cold War, this was peacetime. There was no war except for that business in Vietnam started by Eisenhower, a minor operation that required massive arms but only a small number of American advisors to teach the South how to defend itself from the communist North.

Richie had been scheduled to report in August and never bothered to notify the Board that he'd be absent. Actually he had plumb forgot. Life was too short to worry about some silly induction notice.

Somehow, back in September, the authorities caught up to him on Sullivan Street and were prepared to detain him in some lockup. Richie got on the phone to his dad and got it all straightened out, for the time being.

But time was up. Between the fuzz and the Army, he was cornered. The Army was the obvious way to go.

"Out with it," said Louise.

"What?" Richie laughed.

"You're keeping a secret."

"Never from you, Louise."

"Is it true?"

"Is what true?"

"That the cops came to see you," Louise persisted against Richie's nonchalance.

"Who told you that?"

"Had to be Howie," Ben piped in.

"So is it true?"

"They asked a few questions."

"So tell us what happened," said Louise, truly concerned.

"Nothing happened."

"You're okay?"

"How do I look?" asked Richie, profiling as Barrymore.

"Handsome as ever," said Louise with a glance of feminine delight added to her unique giggle.

Wait till you see me in a uniform, Richie thought. Now that's gonna be something to laugh about.

He simply was not cut out to be a soldier. He was no pacifist, either. Either way was all right so long as they left him alone. He had heard grumblings about something that had nothing to do with him. That Vietnam thing, but that was just people being political and fuck politics.

Some people needed politics and causes to make themselves important - important, confused and idealistic. Not Richie. Keep it light, keep it cool, keep it later man.

Only recently had he begun to realize that people were actually getting *serious*.

Despite Kennedy's pronouncement on Walter Cronkite's evening news that "it is their war," meaning the Vietnamese, and that "we can help them, we can give them equipment, we can send our men out there as advisors, but they have to win it, the people of Vietnam" - despite such disclaimers there was a real risk of war, according to all the talk.

None of which bothered Richie, who actually thought it might be fun to go off to war even though there was no war.

Richie was in a surprisingly reflective mood.

"I think I know what's going on," said Ben.

"What?" said Richie, beginning to soften toward his friend.

"You opened one of the envelopes."

Ben had seen the letters and had even been there when the two military types had come knocking. That was some scene. Ben had been stricken. A knock at the door was a terrible thing. Add two men in military dress and it can only be the Gestapo.

Richie blanched at Ben's mention of the envelopes.

"What envelopes?" said Louise. "Oh, those envelopes you never open and keep telling me they're just 4-F."

"That's right," said Richie, giving Ben a nudge.

"That's right," said Ben.

"Come on you two. What's going on?"

Richie and Ben exchanged a conspiratorial glance.

"Out with it," said Louise.

"No big deal," said Riche. "Just looks like I may end up in Uncle Sam's Army."

Louise laughed. "You're kidding."

"Of course I'm kidding."

"But you keep telling me you never passed the physical."

"That's right. I never passed the physical. Even if I had I'd never go in. Leave you a widow?"

She smiled.

"What would you tell our kids?" Riche said to prolong the joke.

"Huh," she said imperiously. "If you joined the Army you can forget about me. You can forget about kids."

"Now that's strong," said Richie.

"I mean it, Richie, you better be kidding. If you join up, you're gone. I won't think about you for a minute."

"Fair enough. But let's pretend."

"Richie, I don't want to pretend. There's nothing funny about this."

"Well I'm pretending."

"Go ahead, but without me."

"So - would you tell them I died a hero?"

"Who?"

"Our kids."

151

Louise turned grim. "You don't have to die to be my hero. You're already my hero. Same for you, Ben."

The word hero sounded strange to Richie. He wasn't the type. Didn't want to be the type. Heroes were for the movies and his old man's generation. Heroes were outdated. Nowadays heroes weren't hip, they weren't cool. They were square.

His dad, a First Lieutenant in the Marines, had stood his ground under severe Japanese bombardment and after wiping out a pillbox walked away with a Purple Heart and a Silver Star for valor. All of which amounted to a topic of conversation around the dinner table in Hartford. For a while. Then it got boring and nobody talked about it anymore. Then, when it came up for discussion in the presence of Richie's teenage friends, it got downright embarrassing and there was much clearing of throats, even from Mom.

So there was your hero.

God and country. Richie had heard that song and dance from his father, and from his brother, Stephen, a medic who was stationed in Germany during the Berlin Wall crisis and came back to tell Richie about the thrill of expectant combat.

"You ought to go," he told Richie. "Make you a man."

That remark stopped Richie. His own brother did not consider him a man. Despite his experiences, he still did not belong to the club. He had not been tested. He used to think otherwise. But neither his toying with deadly snakes, nor his riding with a Hell's Angels-type motorcycle gang for a month, nor his hitting the road Jack Kerouac-style for six weeks, nor his escapades scuba diving and rock climbing - none of it was sufficient triumph. Combat and only combat was the true measure of a man and so far each living generation but his had been so tested.

He had heard about God and country from Ben as well on the many nights they stayed up together at the Sullivan retreat engaging in bullshit that touched on religion, women, culture, politics, history and anything else that needed to be settled.

Richie was astonished that Ben still believed in God after all that Ben had been through. To believe in a god after the Holocaust was not only naïve, but sacrilegious - a desecration of the martyrs.

"As for me," said Richie, "I believe we created Him, not the other way around."

Ben said, yes, he believed in Him, but, no, that did not mean he wasn't pissed off at Him.

But he was not pissed off on *country*. Ben was rarin' to go. Ready to fight, ready to die.

This also baffled Richie. Richie accused Ben of being a "damned gullible patriot."

"No patriot," said Ben. "Just call me grateful."

Gratitude was a concept completely wacko for a home-grown American like Richie Bell.

"Ben," Richie would say, "you're nuts if you want to join up. You already had your war."

But now Richie was coming around given his choice between a jailhouse tunic and an Army uniform. He was not rarin' to go like Ben. But there seemed no other option and anyway, the Army might be fun and even war might be a kick.

There had to be something to it, given all the literature about the romance and the glory. Hemingway was war. Remarque was war. Tolstoy was war. James Jones was war. Mailer was war. John Wayne, Montgomery Cliff, Burt Lancaster, Gregory Peck, Clark Gable, Jimmy Stewart, Marlene Dietrich, Humphrey Bogart, William Holden, Casablanca, Berlin, Paris - all of it was war and all of it was so romantic.

So Richie was ready.

But World War II, that was the war Richie sought, the kind of war so many young men lusted after. They wanted to liberate the Ritz and make love to Lilli Palmer and then return to America heroic and sullen like Hemingway, and then, like Hemingway, write great novels about their awful and romantic experiences.

Richie was agreeable. But he wanted to suffer stylishly, romantically.

It did not occur to him (not yet, but soon enough) that suffering was undesirable. It couldn't, because he was so American, so utterly, ingenuously American, so unwise, so unknowing about the truth of things.

Europe's wars were America's books and movies. Nobody died except the Nazis and the Japs.

That was the kind of war Richie (and so many others of his generation) expected from the Army. A good, clean, bloodless, heroic war, innocent women and children watching from the sidelines. Nobody gets hurt except the bad guys.

"You're sure you were rejected," said Louise, skepticism beginning to wrinkle her lovely brow.

"Come on, 4-F all the way."

Chapter 21

Again the phone. Gloria picked it up before it could ring a second time and have Cliff throw a fit out there on stage as Shelley Berman once did. Cliff was into a fine rhythm out there and in fact it was one of his best shows. Maybe, she figured, it was for the cameras, or the fact that his cronies were finally in the room - including and especially Lenny Bruce, who kept flipping back and forth from his seat to the john no doubt, thought Gloria, to do some Mary Jane and snort some horse.

So Gloria hastened to the phone before Nate Beloff or Paul Hogan could get to it and who was on the other end of the line? That *shmuck* bastard Arlin Stoner, her ex-husband; ex-husband number one, the insurance salesman. He still had the hots for her and made his awareness known by the oddest pranks. Like now and then, over the years, calling to say that the president had been shot. Running gag, but not very funny, especially not here at the Café Muse, home of the other Kennedy.

Certainly not funny to Gloria, whose entire life and career were wrapped up with Cliff Harris.

That was enough to prompt Arlin.

"Yeah?" she said into the speaker.

Arlin said the president had been shot. "I'm not kidding."

"You prick!" Gloria said hanging up the receiver.

She was steamed. That was a gag she'd never get used to.

"Who was that?" asked Nate.

"That asshole Arlin."

"I know people who can take care of that problem permanently," Nate said half-jokingly.

"I may just enlist you," Gloria said, now sipping a Coke, chewing gum and smoking all at the same time.

She nervously rubbed her bloodshot eyes and sighed and kept a beat on her desk with a ballpoint pen. Her thoughts were on the bomb threat. Nate and Paul had, as usual, bent to her will, but it was a topic that was being discussed here in the back room in silence and averted eyes. Everyone was jumpy.

"What did he want this time?" asked Paul.

"The usual gag."

"That's so cruel," said Nate.

"No, it's just Arlin."

Nate Beloff had a special fear for Jack Kennedy's life. (He certainly had a unique investment.) He was always up six sharp for the news and all he wanted was no news, about the president. Then he'd sigh contentedly and fall back to sleep. His world was safe.

Indirectly and sometimes directly he knew about the threats to Cliff's life, Cliff's as well as the president's. Nate had a pipeline to the Secret Service, or rather an open line. They shared information since a threat on one was as good as a threat on the other.

So Nate had been very cooperative when the Secret Service contacted him after the Bay of Pigs fiasco, and so it was agreed that extra safety measures should be taken since the president's popularity had dipped to a new low and threats to his life had zoomed to a new high.

To Nate it made sense that they work together, he and the federal (and local) authorities - only he sometimes found it amusing that a nightclub owner should be taken so seriously by the Government of the United States of America.

That one time they had even asked him to hand over Cliff Harris' scripts for the government's stamp of approval. That he'd never do, even when questions were raised about the validity of his citizenship papers. He later discovered that the president himself had been outraged by such over-zealous tactics on the part of his palace guards. When word leaked out to the press, that's when Kennedy said, "Besides, that Cliff Harris does me better than I do me." Joe Franklin and Ed Sullivan loved that quote and repeated it numerous times on the air.

"He was kidding of course," said Nate about Arlin.

"Oh, Nate," said Gloria, "you die every night and it isn't even night yet."

"Just checking."

Nate was always just checking. He had that thing called compulsive behavior which had him checking the ash trays a hundred times before he left home and checking the doors the same number of times before he left the club. Around the Village he was known as the Great Worrier.

He was quite handsome in a rugged, rumpled sort of a way, his furrowed brow the map of a hard life.

These days he was worried about things going too well.

By now he knew the Village, that it ebbed and flowed with trends. This too, he thought, shall pass. For it was too good to be true. He was actually making money and this worried him even more than when he wasn't making money.

Just as the moon hid behind the sun, so it was with luck good and bad. He knew the vagaries of fortune from a land-scape of upheaval. He had escaped the pogrom in Russia that had wiped out the rest of his family. Somehow landed in England. For some reason made his way to Palestine.

Fought with the Irgun from 1946 to 1948 when Palestine became Israel. Traveled to America to heal a host of war wounds. Found Hollywood but failed to make it there as an actor or as anything. Arrived in New York just as the folking/hootenanny craze was in its infancy. Saw the opportunity and seized it in the Village.

But it would not last. Nothing lasted. Life was good. Life was bad. Life was bad. Life was good. Then all over again. For some it was all good. So he was unlucky. For some it was all bad. So he was lucky. Then, just when you thought you had it all figured - you figured wrong.

Nate began to pace. "You're sure it was just a gag."

"Nate!" said Gloria, pounding a fist down on her desk.

"Relax," said Paul.

Nate tried to relax and think good thoughts so he thought about the sweet sounds of laughter coming from the packed house out front. He thought about how fortunate he was to have found the comedian who pleased the multitudes. He was on the phone with Ed Sullivan practically every day. Ed Sullivan!

Practically every day the likes of Henny Youngman, Milton Berle, Jack Benny, Jackie Gleason, Red Buttons, Joey Adams, Phil Silvers, came to pay homage and to participate in the show *he* and no one else was putting on.

These giants were, in effect, paying dubious tribute to a new generation even as they were horrified by Richard Pryor and Lenny Bruce and a host of other young upstarts that were replacing the classic one-liner wisecrack with "sick" stream of consciousness comedy, or actually commentary. In their day, in the old days, an "off-color" remark was as far as it went. Even Vaudeville and burlesque had its limits.

In rebuttal they pointed to Bill Cosby and Cliff Harris as upholders of tradition - while making big bucks, too.

Nate Beloff had their gratitude, and with Cliff Harris Nate Beloff had it both ways - young and old.

Now he was successful and rich and now he was worried.

Again the phone.

"If that's Arlin I'll kill him," said Gloria.

But it wasn't Arlin. It was Patrolman Ornstein. He wanted to know why Cliff's show was still going on. Had Howie told her the news? Yes, Ornstein knew the show biz imperative *the show must go on* but this was different! If ever a show needed to be stopped, this was the show.

Gloria had never heard such a strange question. "Why shouldn't it go on?" she asked belligerently.

"Haven't you heard?"

"Heard what?"

"Didn't Howie tell you?"

"Tell me what?"

"The news that John Kennedy was dead."

Gloria said nothing. There was nothing much to say after a booby-trap just exploded in your face.

"I mean of all places to be laughing when the whole world is crying," said Ornstein. "I mean, you people more than..."

Gloria wasn't listening anymore. In the shock of the moment she had felt her body go numb. Her limbs weakened to the point of collapse and the knot in her stomach was quickly turning to nausea. No, she thought. NO NO NO! Please. NO! But finally - it happened. Yes it did. Yes it did. But she was a quick study. She was tough. Not for nothing was she Tough As Nails Gloria, and that meant expect the best and be prepared for the worst. This was the worst. So it was time to be a soldier and dig in.

She gave herself a few moments to subdue her emotions, then, after the shock subsided, she moved swiftly into damage control, which led her to the conclusion that she would be no catalyst to set off a chain of events; rather, she reasoned, let events sort themselves out and dictate the shape of things.

This was not a time to lead, it was a time to be led by circumstances. The moment demanded inaction; that would be the true test of courage and wisdom. To yell THE PRESIDENT IS DEAD in a crowded theater, and not just any theater, but a theater that was poking fun at the president, good-natured though it was, would cause panic to everlasting.

People would never forget that this was where they heard it first, that this was where it happened. They would forever associate the death of the president with Cliff Harris and the Café Muse.

This she would not allow.

So if the party had to end, as obviously it did, let it end outside, after the show. Let the wind carry the news. Not Cliff, not Gloria, not Nate, not Paul. No, not from this arena would go forth the word.

"Anything?" asked Nate Beloff about the latest phone call.

"The usual," said Gloria.

Chapter 22

Cliff was beginning to toil. Though they were still lapping it up and demanding more moments from the album his delivery had begun to wither. He was stale and he was floundering. He had only so much left anyway and it was usually at around this juncture that he'd prepare to bow and make his exit. But Lenny Bruce was here and Lenny had never heard his take on the dark side of America, never heard him do *Cliff Harris* - never on stage, before an audience, before cameras. Same for Ben and Richie and Louise and Sonny and Joe Franklin, that whole gang that loved him as a copycat but had no regard for him as an original. They had never seen him perform publicly as a man with sharp personal observations. This, then, was the moment to make the dramatic switch to free association and present his bitter view of the other America, which would mean dropping the Kennedy mask of benevolence in exchange of a malevolent actually grotesque caricature of the president.

Sonny Schwartz saw it coming. Cliff had paused during the improvisational question and answer period and failed to respond as Kennedy when asked his opinion about an embargo on Cuba. The usual comeback went something like: "Jackie never lets me smoke those cigahs around the-ah White House anyway." This time, however, Cliff showed no trace of a Kennedy grin. His face turned hard around the edges as he said, "Peace, man," and held up the peace sign.

Sonny rushed to Lenny's table and whispered, "Stop him!"

Lenny was floating on horse but he agreed that this was neither the time or the place. Or the man. Cliff Harris was not the man to do the job. Cliff was not the man to do Lenny Bruce. There was only one Lenny Bruce and that was enough, if not too much.

In fact - a fact that escaped the authorities and much of the public - Lenny Bruce was downright conventional in his deference to ethics and outright sentimental in his love of country.

That, indeed, was what motivated him to take the stage as a deranged (but accurate and truthful) Biblical prophet, following the footsteps of Jeremiah whose Lamentations spoke words of brutal truth to a nation in the advanced stages of decay. Jeremiah foresaw a "river of tears" for a kingdom on the eve of destruction - ditto Lenny Bruce.

His supporters, rather his disciples, equated him with Jesus Christ. His detractors, most vehemently the police and the courts and the religious right, referred to him as Satan. To these foes, he epitomized the evils sweeping America.

The fag culture, the drug scene, the profanity craze, the anti-Government anti-Establishment anti-God anti-Mom anti-apple pie movement, all were thought to begin and end at his feet; precisely the attributes that prompted his followers to declare him the Second Coming.

A myth and a legend even in advance of his universal fame, he had made it to TV via the *Steve Allen Show*, but few other live variety showcases would chance him. He was so unpredictable.

He could begin clean and sober enough - he sure looked decent and well-mannered if a bit too Semitic - and then suddenly veer off into dangerous territory. There was no telling what he might say or when he might let loose his *Seven Forbidden Words.*

The herald of reason, the voice of doom, the chronicler of America's hypocrisies, the piper of every weirdo yearning to be heard, the promoter of sex between everybody, the exponent of pot, cocaine and heroin, the advocate of all that was hidden and shameful, the champion of excess, he was, Jesus Christ or otherwise, the prophet that America both scorned and adored.

The police and the courts, acting as surrogates for the nation, were determined to muzzle and stop him for the preservation of the American Way and for the safety of America's sons and daughters. He was the antithesis of Kennedy. He was the anti-Kennedy.

While barely in his prime, he had already endured harassment and imprisonment from coast to coast, largely due to the profanities he engaged in on stage and the drugs he inhaled, injected, snorted, licked off stage.

All in the same breath he feared the Establishment and provoked it to test the limits of America's freedom and America's patience for someone who was too far out even during these days of hipness.

America feared that he may be the future. (He was). To the right he was the precursor of youth gone mad, a generation about to go berserk on sex, drugs and rock & roll. The left saw his opponents, mainly the fuzz, as being the harbinger of nationwide oppression.

In private he was cordial, interested and interesting, though always brooding, restless and intense. He was a member in good standing of the Roundtable at McSorley's but was not a regular. Occasionally he stopped by the Sullivan retreat to partake in the household delicacies, namely the women, and once made an unsuccessful move on Louise Carmen.

Given to frequent migraines, he sought comfort in Richie's music, of all things. Richie did have magic in the living room and Lenny would drift off as Richie strummed and hummed Judy Collin's mournful "Anathea."

Among companions he was anything but the wild man. Lacking formal education (much of his knowledge came from his years in the Navy), he lusted for wisdom, always quizzing Richie and Ben and Cliff and Louise and Harlan English (the sometime black visitor to Sullivan Street), and demanding to know everything about their lives.

He wanted to know what it was like to be a Jew in Europe, a Negro in America, a rich kid from Connecticut, an entertainer from Philadelphia, a woman in the 60s, a fag, a pimp, a hustler, a junkie, all the things, he said, that made this country great through diversity, while the fuzz were busy pissing in the melting pot.

He took notes. Everything was useful as material. He'd lean back and wonder if Dwight ever made love to Mamie and during the free association that followed among the irregulars a new routine was born.

Sometimes he'd concede that he was tired of the whole business, tired of being the scapegoat - but, that was his role and there was no stopping destiny.

He had lived too much in so short a time. (Before making it in the Biz, and starving, he had passed himself off as a clergyman collecting donations for some charity overseas. Dressed as a priest, he went door to door soliciting funds from old ladies who gave gladly to such a worthy cause. He was finally busted, but did indeed send a considerable portion of his ill-gotten earnings to the charity he had so fraudulently represented.)

He was tired and disillusioned, disillusioned at what passed for Authority in America, particularly religious institutions and their Legions of Decency that were constantly monitoring and hassling him and that were so concerned about the allures of the female breast and not at all concerned about relieving human suffering. A statement he made at McSorley's found its way directly into his autobiographical "How to Talk Dirty and Influence People."

"It's a girlie magazine was all that was left as a document of this generation, an anthropologist of the year 2001 would logically assume that this culture seemed to be identified with the religious concept: 'God made my body and if it is dirty, then the imperfection lies with the Manufacturer, not the product. Do not remove this tag under penalty of law.'"

He admitted that he was frightened. The fuzz were tormenting him. He had no choice but to torment them back but he knew who would win in the end. "It won't be Lenny Bruce," he said. (He died three years later, August 3, 1966, of an overdose of drugs after losing a thousand battles against the fuzz, the courts, his addiction, his ex-wife Honey.)

He loved all women and the woman he loved most loved him least. That was Honey.

He was seldom funny in private and claimed not to be funny even in public.

"I'm not a comedian, man. It's not *funny* what's going on out there."

"So what are you?" Ben would ask.

"I'm a fucking moralist."

He was a fucking moralist trying to get America off its false values.

"I'm fucking serious," he said. "You know why they laugh? Because I'm serious, dig?"

More than anything, he wanted to be a novelist. His work in progress, "How to Talk Dirty and Influence People," was not coming along. Cliff was helping with his *goyishe* perspective on things, but Lenny wanted more and more shit to fill the pages and was constantly after Richie - "you're my Harvard man" - to recommend books he ought to be reading. Richie's list included D.H. Lawrence, Hemingway, Fitzgerald, Proust, Twain, Montaigne.

Why Montaigne? Because like Lenny Bruce, Montaigne was an essayist - if far more subtle.

"Subtlety works," said Richie.

"Not in this country it doesn't. In this country you've got to hit people over the head."

But one day Lenny Bruce arrived with all the books Richie had recommended and spent a full week hidden away in the back bedroom reading them cover to cover. Without mentioning it, he was also, at the moment, in hiding from the Mob.

He had the fuzz chasing him through one door, the Mob through the other.

"Good shit," he said about his reading orgy. "But they're all fags."

"Hemingway?"

"Yeah, all that *fakate* violence. No wonder. I mean, man, the love of the kill? That's the moment of truth? Can't say fuck in public, can't say shit, piss, motherfucker, cunt, orgasm, masturbate, but man, how we love violence. Murder - that's not a forbidden word. Hey, Hemingway's exactly what I'm crusading *against*!"

On this day at the Café Muse Lenny had arrived and was seated with his usual consort of fruits and other undesirables. He was attired like any overly-sharp tourist; silk suit, white shirt and black tie. His soulful almond-shaped eyes kept darting around the room. He was a vision in black, a blur of darkness, a figure of agitation as he kept fidgeting in his seat.

He agreed with Sonny. This was not the time or the place and Cliff Harris was not the man. The nation and this audience would accept only so many malcontents. Blistering humor belonged to the chosen few, the exiled.

"I have a question, Mr. President," Lenny began, emphasizing *Mr. President.*

Cliff was thrilled. "We-ah seem to have another question. Yes, sir. What would you-ah like to know?"

"Mr. President, what's your position on sex?"

Titters from the audience.

"Only Hugh-ah Hefner knows all the-ah positions," Cliff responded on cue. "Any other questions, sir?"

Then it happened - and so swiftly. Three men in brown suits got up, moved in on Lenny Bruce, surrounded him and escorted him to the lobby where they handcuffed him, Lenny put up no resistance. This was business as usual, another day at the office. Someone in the audience had yelled out: "They can't do this. This is America." Later, in the paddy wagon, Lenny mumbled: "They keep forgetting."

Chapter 23

The contretemps broke Cliff's spirit, but he was a pro, a trooper, but now, deviating from the prepared narrative, he spoke out as if he were the real president, declaring that, as President of the United States, he could "not permit such lawlessness on the part of the law." The terrible thing that had just happened, he said, was a perversion of justice, a violation to the Constitution, a mockery of the Fourth Amendment which guaranteed the right of the people to be secure in their persons and homes. The same Amendment defended the people against unreasonable searches and seizures.

All of which had just taken place, he said, before our very eyes.

A good portion of the audience - mainly the tourists - thought this was still part of the act and were prepared to laugh and when Cliff heard one such guffaw he glared at the offender and said, "Shut up!" This led to queasy silence.

Cliff had more. "You think this is funny? You came for the jokes? What you just saw was no joke."

Yes, he went on, real life happens even here in Greenwich Village, the toy department of the nation.

Now, he said, addressing the tourists, the squares, the Iowans, the Ohioans, the Nebraskans, the Coloradans, the Texans, the Carolinians, and all the rest of the squares and hayseeds from the heartland who had come for the joyride -

now, he said bitterly, you see what we mean by oppression. What happened to Lenny Bruce - yes, ladies and gentlemen, that was Lenny Bruce - what happened to Lenny Bruce could happen to you, you and you. You are not safe. Not in your homes. Not in public places. Beware of the words you use. Someone is listening.

In homage to Lenny, Cliff was prepared to utter the *Seven Forbidden Words.* But he forgot them for the moment. Or maybe, he thought, I am too chicken. Time, he thought, to stop being chicken.

He asked for silence as he recited the following: "*fuck, shit, piss, motherfucker, cunt, orgasm, masturbate.*"

Then he announced: "That was for Lenny and all advocates of freedom of expression."

The people did not know what to make of this. They were shocked but prepared to let it slide.

Their devotion to him was still too strong to be slackened by a temporary failing.

Without meaning to make the switch at this moment, but triggered by the seizure of Lenny Bruce, Cliff managed to turn himself into the grotesque messenger of truth that had been his plan all along. He was furious that the American netherworld of Joseph McCarthy and Roy Cohn and Richard Nixon had reared its ugly head in such a public place at such a public moment, all in the presence of the President of the United States.

In other words, Cliff had lost it; he had snapped, gone over the edge, gone berserk. The ego and alter ego, the fake and the real, the phony and the genuine, had finally merged so that he was deluded into believing himself to be the actual John F. Kennedy. Yes, he was John F. Kennedy, but he would rule with the soul and the dictates of Lenny Bruce.

Now he abruptly exited stage left before a stunned audience and stormed into Gloria's office to demand that she convene an immediate special session of Congress where he, Cliff Harris, acting as president, or rather, no longer *acting* as president, could denounce the police, the military, the Pentagon, the FBI, the CIA - the Establishment in its oppressive entirety.

Gloria was enraged by Cliff's apostasy, but long-suffering Paul Hogan was merely saddened. This day had been waiting to happen. There had been just one other time when Cliff had turned delusional and fused his split personality, but that was when he had been hallucinating from a dose of cocaine, a drug he never used - never used drugs period - but had given it a try when Howie, in the name of Lenny Bruce, accused him of being square.

Maybe, Paul reasoned, he'd done it again, this time to get himself pumped for the *sick shtick* he was proposing to unload, according to the grapevine. In any case, Paul blamed himself, not only for this awful moment, but for the whole thing, the whole mixed up thing that was Cliff Harris/John Kennedy.

He, Paul Hogan, had created a hybrid and now, here was the disastrous result.

This man needed not fame, not fortune, not adulation. He did not need Ed Sullivan, or the Café Muse, or the millions who adored him and hungered for his next Kennedyesque utterance. This man needed *therapy*. For three years now he'd been spliced in half, teetering between himself and his alter ego, and he needed to be put back together again.

Gloria took no time for such deliberations. She slapped Cliff across the face, grabbed him by the shoulders until he finally regained his senses, more or less, though in his eyes there was still a glint of insanity.

"What did you do that for?" Cliff snapped.

"You're tripping, Cliff. Get yourself together, boy, there's worse."

"Did you see what just happened? Lenny Bruce..."

Gloria said that was nothing. Nate and Paul were surprised to hear this. Their club had just been profaned.

What could be worse?

"The president is dead," said Gloria.

Cliff, now partly lucid and beginning to regain his equilibrium, asked for the punch line.

No punch line, said Gloria. The president is dead.

"Kennedy?" said Nate, gasping and choking on his saliva.

"No more Kennedy," said Gloria. "The president is Johnson."

Yes, Gloria admitted, she had known it for nearly an hour but had kept it to herself to avert a panic and to allow the show to run its course and to keep the Café Muse, and that's you Cliff, and you Nate, and you Paul, from being forever associated and tainted with the tragedy; stigmatized with the most horrific single moment in this American century.

"When did this happen?" asked a stricken Paul Hogan.

"He died more than an hour ago."

"Where?" asked Nate.

"In Dallas."

Gloria then passed along the details. Patrolman Ornstein had provided an item-by-item account.

"This is not real," said Nate.

"What do we tell the people out there?" asked Paul.

"We tell them the truth. The show is over."

"Who's gonna tell them?" asked Nate.

Gloria turned to Cliff with an uncompromising gaze. "You'll have to tell them, Cliff."

Cliff stood there mute and petrified.

"Wake up, Cliff! You've got a job to do."

"This is not real," Nate said again, as if saying it again and again it would turn out to be false.

But Nate was not really shocked. He had half expected this, someday, someplace, somehow. Never, though, had he expected it in the middle of a Cliff Harris performance. Never. No god could not be that cruel. But here it was. The moment was here, that moment he dreaded each morning. Here it was.

Not that he was thinking of himself and his personal loss. He was thinking of the country. No pretender to the throne could come close to duplicating the magic of Kennedy.

This kind of a leader came along once in a century. For wit, depth of character, charisma, there had been nothing like him since Thomas Jefferson. The words of the psalmist *"why art thou downcast o' my soul"* came to him when he realized what Gloria had just said. Lyndon Johnson. President Lyndon Johnson. How dissonant it all sounded. Lyndon Johnson, president. The torch was being passed to Lyndon Johnson.

Nate's following thought - all of which came tumbling in a flash - was of Cliff.

My God! Cliff!

Cliff was finished.

Cliff was dead, too.

The same Lenny Bruce who had been arrested just moments ago had uttered that very prophecy about two graves at Arlington. Make room for two graves at Arlington if Kennedy goes down. Lenny Bruce, the prophet. John Kennedy, the president. No, Lyndon Johnson, the president.

For an instant Nate gave way to a selfish thought. Well, he'd go on. He always did. Hollywood was his next stop anyway. There was always something else. That was the trouble. Always something else. Always something pursuing him, from the czar to this.

But he felt no pity for himself. He was not jinxed. The nation was jinxed. The world was jinxed.

"Figures to be Dallas," said Paul, emerging from his own catatonia. "Isn't Johnson from Texas?"

"Don't," said Gloria, the only level-headed member of the group. "No time for backsliding. Cliff, let's go!"

"I can't," said Cliff. "I can't go out there."

"Maybe I should go," said Nate. "This is my club."

"But they're Cliff's people," said Gloria.

"That's true," said Paul.

"But they're *not* my people," protested Cliff. "Not anymore."

That was also true. Very true. So very true. Now they were Lyndon Johnson's people.

"No it can't be Cliff," said Paul, coming to the defense of his boy. "They'll hate him now until doomsday."

"*This is doomsday,*" Gloria reminded the gathering.

"I'll do it," said Cliff.

"I'll go with you," said Nate.

"Break a leg," said Paul.

"That's bad luck," said Cliff.

"You mean it can get any worse?" said Nate.

Together Cliff and Nate marched out and faced the people. The people applauded. Cliff was forgiven his outburst. Perhaps unprofessional, but only natural that a man should lose his composure when a member of his audience is suddenly plucked up and removed.

The people were ready for Cliff's take on Khrushchev's shoe-pounding tantrum at the United Nations. That was the hit of the album. The people knew the album by heart. They knew what came next.

Nate held up his arms in a call for silence and except for some titters of expectation, there was silence.

Nate did not know how to frame the words. He stood speechless and motionless.

How does one break the news?

How can it be done to land softly? Here of all places.

Was there any way to say it besides saying *the president is dead*?

No, there was no other way. Those were the only words.

Nate tried to open by saying there is bad news.

The people thought it was part of the performance and interrupted him with belly laughs.

"No," Nate said. "This is bad news - and please, do not rush the exits."

A fire?

"Ladies and gentlemen," Nate began - but he could not finish.

A heckler demanded that Nate get off the stage. "Let's have Cliff. Let's have Kennedy."

"There is no Kennedy," said Nate. "That's the news."

"What the hell is that supposed to mean?" another heckler shouted.

"The president is dead," said Nate.

"That's not funny," came a chorus from the back.

"Ladies and gentlemen," said Nate, "we received word that John Kennedy was assassinated in Dallas."

For the sake of authenticity, Nate explained that Jack and Jackie Kennedy were riding in a motorcade in downtown Dallas early this afternoon. They were in an open car. At 1:30 this afternoon, something like an hour ago, shots rang out from a building, known as the Texas School Book Depository. Three bullets hit the president.

The president and Texas Governor John B. Connally, who was riding in the same car and was also struck, were rushed to Parkland Memorial Hospital. The president never regained consciousness. He was declared dead at 2 p.m.

The people refused to believe.

"The president is dead."

This, they reasoned (or prayed), was part of the set up for a Cliff Harris zinger. No such luck.

Now they believed and gasped as one. Women began to weep openly. There were wails of grieving.

Someone begged Cliff to say it ain't so.

"Please, everybody go home," said Nate. "The show is over."

"You bet!" came a catcall.

"Please leave orderly," said Nate as there was a rush for the doors. Some people were running for cover, imagining assassins all over the room, all over the nation. Now suddenly - in the grip of terror - your neighbor could be a killer.

Some people remained. They stayed to study this parvenu that was Cliff. They stayed to vilify him.

Somehow, he was at fault. He had betrayed them. Kennedy was dead but Cliff Harris was alive. Why?

"You're dead, too," came a taunt.

"Why weren't you in Dallas?" came another.

The *Seven Forbidden Words* came back to haunt Cliff.

"Fuck."

"Shit."

"Piss."

"Motherfucker."

"Cunt."

"Orgasm."

"Masturbate."

Those words echoed brutally across the room from the laggards who remained to taunt.

A group wearing black leather jackets began a menacing move toward the stage.

That's when Cliff lost it again and said that he was still here, Kennedy was still here, very much alive.

Nate grabbed him by the arms and tried to rush him off stage before more damage was done. But Cliff resisted. He had more material. He was not done. "I'm not done," he roared at Nate. "I'm not finished."

"Yes you are," said Nate.

Chapter 24

What's next? What could possibly be next? That was the question baffling the shell-shocked foursome of Cliff, Richie, Ben, and Louise. They were the last to leave the Café Muse and as they stepped out onto Bleecker gone were the crowds except for Lobo the Prophet running naked and howling up at the sky. Otherwise they beheld an earth as in the Beginning when all was unformed and void and darkness was upon the face of the deep.

Patrolmen Ornstein and Massaria were on hand to provide security for Cliff, but Cliff declined their assistance. Anyhow the place was rich with cops mounted and on foot patrol, which only made the scene all the more desolate and strange.

Cliff's "Thank You, Mr. President" album was littered across the doorpost of the Café Muse as the multitudes that had come for autographs dispersed in disgust and revulsion and wanted no trace of Cliff or the occasion.

The record had been smashed to bits along the streets and sidewalks; reminders of it in front of the Back Fence on Bleecker and Sullivan, the Feenjon and the Village Gate on Bleecker and MacDougal, the Bijou on Third, the Pink Pussycat on Fourth - and more debris at the Bitter End, the Café Wha, the Dugout, McSorley's and throughout Sheridan and Washington Square Park. The people were making a statement.

To Ben, it was something like the Kristallnacht, that rampage in Germany that preceded and foreshadowed the Holocaust.

By the time they reached their Sullivan Street hideaway, the President of the United States was indeed Lyndon Johnson, seen taking the oath of office on television next to a stricken and blood-soaked Jackie Kennedy. Johnson was sworn in at 3:38 p.m. aboard Air Force One.

Howie had beaten them to the apartment and was quick to inform Cliff that phone calls had already come in cancelling him on Ed Sullivan and the 12 clubs that had extended offers. Corporations and universities had called to inform him that he was being deleted from commercials and speeches. His album was being pulled from the record stores all across the country.

"Leave it to Howie to break the news," said Richie, shaking his head in disgust.

"What?" protested Howie. "It's not my fault."

"No, Howie," said Ben. "Just seems that way."

"Leave him alone," said Louise. "We don't need more ugliness."

Louise Carmen was not young anymore. Then again, nobody was.

The past couple of hours had accelerated the aging process by leaps.

Harlan English arrived and they surrounded him and hugged him and now, for the first time since that terrible moment, they all wept, Louise most bitterly of all. They needed to weep and found the pretext in Harlan because he was black and had frequently predicted more than strife, but outright war between the races if Kennedy ever went down. Kennedy was just keeping the lid over a simmering caldron.

He too had walked the desolate streets of this Friday, November 22nd and was spooked.

A gang of thugs had already pursued him with epithets.

"This is the beginning of the end," he said as they sat there glumly watching the latest on television. "Hatred is in the air. There's fuzz all over the place. It's bad, just plain bad. I'm moving to France. There's never been a lynching in France."

Harlan, a jazz musician at the Village Gate, was one of those who drifted in and out of the Sullivan Street household. He gave the joint dignity, Richie often said. Harlan had a degree from Princeton.

What's more, Harlan was soft-spoken and deliberate in his actions. He was a gentleman of the old school, the heir to a New Jersey department store fortune. "I feel it in my bones," he said of the onrushing apocalypse.

Months ago at an uptown tavern the bartender refused to serve "that nigger" a brew. Ben and Richie appealed to the owner, the bouncer, the patrons and after politeness failed they commenced to rip the place apart. The slugfest and the bruises they had to show for it later made them blood brothers.

But not completely. Even the bar fight - which they had clearly won in Three Musketeers style against a roomful of goons - was no victory in Harlan's eyes. No, just more of the same and a reminder of the battles that loomed ahead. In the end, it would be white against black, and no Ben and Richie to the rescue.

Ben was especially puzzled by Harlan. This racial thing was so uniquely American. You had to be born here to understand. Where he came from it was all about ethnicity and geography and tyrants. But here it was something in the soil and you had to be born in America to know how it had been planted and how it was harvested.

In the America Ben had settled into Negroes were either invisible or happy men and women, happy to be porters, maids, street cleaners, musicians, tap dancers, Amos and Andy and "Yezzuh Mister Benny." Not until rather later in his American Experience had Ben awakened to the knowledge that Negroes were not happy being "Negroes."

None of this was bigotry on Ben's part. It was simply the America he had inherited.

Negroes shined shoes. Negroes danced for pennies outside Crosley Field in Cincinnati during the Red's baseball games. Shuffle them feet, white men said. You people don't have it in the head, but you sho do have it in the legs, white women said.

The Negroes kept on dancing throughout Ben's American apprenticeship of the 1950s.

But now it was the 1960s and *Blacks* were raising their fists. Harlan spoke frequently about black being beautiful. He had begun referring to black women as *sisters* and black men as *brothers*.

Changes are coming, Harlan said, and it won't be pretty. He was right.

Blacks and whites were squaring off in the streets even with Kennedy in the White House. Freedom Riders were getting beaten up in the South. Black Power was taking root. Sides were being chosen. Kennedy's New Frontier meant nothing to Harlan.

The New Frontier, as everything else in America, was a white man's frontier. America's friends, as always, were a white man's friends. America's enemies were a white man's enemies.

Blacks had no grievance with Russia. Those were white capitalists Khrushchev kept threatening to bury. Not black slaves. Harlan could not muster the necessary affection for

America's European friends nor the requisite invective against America's traditional enemies.

Harlan astonished Ben when he said he had nothing against the Russians.

He confounded even Richie when he declared that during Western movies he, and all blacks, sided with the Indians.

He said America had a crush on John Kennedy but was secretly courting George ("Segregation today, segregation tomorrow, segregation forever") Wallace. Think of *The Picture of Dorian Gray*, he said. There's two sides to every man, every nation.

That was Harlan who gave Lenny Bruce a cigarette at the Café Au Go Go and it was Lenny Bruce who made this historic remark from the stage: "Shit, this smoke was nigger-lipped."

Harlan knew Lenny and he knew the purpose of the joke but he'd begun to wonder if such blasphemy really shocked people to their senses as opposed to having the contrary effect of sedating them into accepting such terms. (Was Lenny Bruce really immunizing America with his *Seven Forbidden Words*, as was his stated intention, or was the masturbating, motherfucker merely teaching the kids a new vocabulary?)

America was hurting.

John Kennedy would be the savior. John Kennedy was the future.

Now John Kennedy was the past.

Three bullets did it; turned the future into the past, turned the dream into a nightmare.

And how long did it take? About two seconds. And how long ago did this happen?

Days? Weeks? Months?

No, hours ago.

"I'm going out for cold cuts," said Louise as the others sat paralyzed in front of the TV - that black and white TV set that no one in this apartment had ever bothered with before. Who cared what was happening *outside*?

Louise brought back bagel, salami, corned beef and Pepsi from Katz's Deli on Houston. She reported that it was spooky out on the streets. Doors bolted and cops everywhere. The sound of horses' hooves gave her the creeps. She loved the sound, but on gravel, not on asphalt.

"It's like a foreign country out there," she said. "Or like there's been an invasion or something."

She phoned her mother. Her mother asked her if she was all right. "Of course I'm all right," Louise said, being the big girl that she was and not a baby her mother still thought her to be. She wanted her daughter to come home to Wheeling. I'll be there when the tour takes me there, that's in a few days - but not before. "But you're in New York," her mother moaned. "You know what can happen in New York." Louise straightened her out fast. "Mom, Kennedy was killed in *Dallas*, remember?" Yes, not in the big bad East, but in the heartland!

Richie called his mom and dad in Hartford and had pretty much the same conversation.

Everybody wanted to know if everybody was safe.

They ate the sandwiches Louise had prepared in the kitchen. They ate and watched TV and now the name Lee Harvey Oswald began to dominate the top stories. There was mention of a wider conspiracy. There was talk that all government officials were marked for assassination. Police were on alert throughout the nation. People were warned not to panic. That caused people to panic. There was a run on supermarkets to stock up on food in case the Soviets took the opportunity to attack.

Lee Harvey Oswald. All three networks mentioned him as the assassin and, Ben noted to the gathering, there seemed to be an obsession in nailing the killer. Richie said, "And why not?"

Ben said, "Perfectly proper. Except that they seem to think by naming the killer somehow that'll be justice. Can't bring Kennedy back to life so the emphasis has to be on something, so I guess this is as good as anything. I just think it's like a substitute, like a diversion to rally us into believing that if we just get this guy everything will be all right.

"Or like an elixir to sedate us. Like we need *something, anything*, to keep us busy, keep our minds off what really happened. Kennedy is dead. That's what happened. They're trying to divert us. But it's human nature. Get the killer and we all feel better. That's the idea. Am I making any sense?"

"No," said Richie.

"Yes," said Louise. "Takes our minds off the shock being so preoccupied with that guy."

Lee Harvey Oswald.

Pedestrians were being interviewed by newsmen and asked where they were when they first heard the news.

For some reason that was important. As if that too were a tonic.

On CBS a woman said: "This is so awful, and I wonder what'll happen to that other guy, you know, Cliff Harris."

Nobody turned to Cliff and Cliff pretended not to hear the remark. But he heard it and was sickened. Not for himself but for the chutzpah of such a concern in the gut of a nation's grieving.

He got up and went to the bathroom and could be heard retching. Then he went to one of the bedrooms for some shuteye, or simply to remove himself even from the company of friends and most certainly from the uncompromising severity of television.

Facts upon facts, faces upon faces, voices upon voices - it all began to blur and sound like mockery. The harpies were gnashing their teeth and screeching and preparing a net to ensnare him. He took a bottle with him to bed.

The rest of them stayed put with TV. The nation had come to an abrupt halt and whatever was happening was happening on TV, and there was a collective comfort in it, to remember that America was a family, a dysfunctional, grieving family, but a family.

All over America people took part in this pastime and from this time onward America never stopped watching TV. (This was where the glassy-eyed compulsion took root.) The millions were still waiting for a surprise. The president was not dead after all. The doctors had made a mistake. But no such word was forthcoming from Walter Cronkite or from Huntley and Brinkley. No, John Kennedy was dead. That would never change.

Gloria MacKenzie arrived. She ran to Richie and hugged him. Then she hugged Louise and called her "my poor baby." She hugged Ben. She hugged Harlan and asked for Cliff. He'd need the biggest hug of all.

"Better do it now," Harlan said, "because after this we're all on our own."

Chapter 25

In the days, weeks and months that followed practically everything that was nailed down was named John Kennedy. Cape Canaveral became Cape Kennedy. Idlewild Airport became Kennedy Airport. Streets, schools, cultural centers, hospitals named or renamed themselves Kennedy.

Only Lyndon Johnson could not rename himself Kennedy. A sick joke - and this was a time for sick jokes - making the rounds from Berkeley to Greenwich Village ran as follows: Lee Harvey Oswald, where are you now that we need you?

Snow began to fall and Greenwich Village was covered in waves of glistening whiteness. Louise was gone, gone on tour with the Highlight Singers as promised and threatened. Richie was gone. Richie was in the Army now. Yes Richie was in the Army. He was laughing his way through basic training and soon he'd be laughing his way to Vietnam.

Louise never had a chance to say goodbye and she'd never believe it; Richie in the Army. He had lied about being 4-F all the way. He was 1-A all the way, all the way to the front.

Ben was in the Navy and he hadn't lied. Weeks after his visit to the recruitment center in Times Square she had confronted Ben with a direct question. Was he being drafted by the Navy? No, he said. He was not being drafted. He was *enlisting*. He did not tell her that part.

She never got a chance to say goodbye to him, either. She was on tour and had a career of her own.

Harlan left for Chicago to try out for the orchestra. He wanted to be a classical musician, his degree from Princeton in liberal arts notwithstanding. Howie was still around seeking new companions, new contacts, a new Lenny Bruce.

Lenny Bruce was in California getting busted every other day. Nate Beloff sold most of his interest in the Café Muse to Gloria MacKenzie and he was now in Hollywood. Another stop for Nate and maybe this would be the final one.

Gloria was determined to stick to the Village. This was home. She was headlining a new comedic find named Peter Hayes. She had auditioned numerous comedians and settled on Peter Hayes because he wasn't vulgar and didn't do impressions.

She'd never go back to that again, even though comedian David Frye was gaining national attention through his impersonation of Lyndon Johnson - but it wasn't the same.

Now the people were laughing at the president's boorishness, his clumsy attempts to be folksy.

But Gloria would have none of that, an act that literally lived and died with the president.

Once was enough and no JFK or Cliff Harris would ever come around again.

Cliff moved full-time to his apartment uptown. He had saved enough money to begin life as a recluse. He was mapping strategy for a comeback, but on his own terms. This time he would show them his real stuff. Meanwhile he boozed and watched TV and was afraid to walk the streets.

People blanched and did double-takes when they saw him. They were horrified by the sight of him. He was a ghost. He wad dead but he was alive; he was alive but he was dead.

He was the image of a dream gone to nightmare, of good gone sour.

So he hid from the public, but in disguise he became a fixture at the racetrack, where he kept losing. His old flame from the Main Line of Philadelphia visited him and planned to stay but she was frightened off by his moods.

He raged at fate and the human condition. He actually told her to leave. He did not want pity, he did not want love, he did not want anything. He just wanted his bottle, his horses and to be left alone. Fuck the world.

In desperation he did try Sullivan and Sullivan wouldn't even pick up the phone.

Sullivan told Paul Hogan that he never wanted to hear that voice or that name. Never again. Cliff was poison.

Cliff was disgraced and was about to be obliterated.

Paul kept trying to book him but they all said the same thing. Cliff was poison. Don't even mention the name.

Cliff tried Gloria again. Certainly not as JFK. But as Cliff Harris.

Not in a million years, said Gloria. Besides, business was terrible. Do you see any people? asked Gloria.

No, there were no people.

Greenwich Village was closed.

Chapter 26

Ben was proud to wear the Navy uniform. It stamped him a true American, if fraudulently so since a uniform was nothing without valor. He had portraits taken of himself in full seaman's dress to show his wife and kids. But whoever they turned out to be, they'd surely be proud. The portraits of him in an American military uniform were for his parents as well. They were dead but he knew they were watching. They had spared him from the death camps of Europe and behold the result! Their son, an American, an American soldier. From the ovens of Dachau to the decks of the U.S.S. Saratoga in a span of but 20 years! Incredible.

He reported for boot camp the latter part of March 1964 and did his 10 weeks in Great Lakes outside of Chicago. As an enlisted man he had a choice to go to specialty school, but he already had a specialty, and that was journalism. Those three and a half years at Ohio State, fractured as they were, now came in handy.

As a journalist, third class petty officer, JO3, he was assigned to Washington to write for the Navy's *All Hands* magazine. This was not what he had expected; a desk job while something was going on out there in Vietnam. Nothing big, but at least there he might see action and action was what he wanted.

So he bitched and got everybody pissed off. But he prevailed and got the transfer to the U.S.S. Valcour, one of three small seaplane tenders. These were ships that tended to seaplanes and the Valcour was setting out for the Arab nation of Bahrain. Sounded good enough to Ben.

Ben reported to Norfolk as ordered and got there just moments before the ship got underway. He bunked in and waited, then waited some more along with the rest of the sailors, all of whom wondered what the delay was all about.

Finally an announcement came over the horn: "Now here this. This man Jaffa lay down the personnel office."

Me? Thought Ben. Me? Out of all these men, me? What did I do?

Turned out he didn't do anything - besides being Jewish. "You're Jewish, aren't you," said the personnel officer. Ben said yes he was and what did that have to do with anything? Well, the Arabs have an agreement with the United States prohibiting Jewish sailors, or Jewish soldiers of any sort, from stepping foot on Arab territory.

Sorry. But can't go with you on board.

"So now where do I go?" said Ben.

Since the personnel officer could not issue direct orders, he gave Ben a verbal order to report to the Valcour's sister ship, the U.S.S. Greenwich Bay that was in dry dock in Portsmouth. This ship was also set to sail for Bahrain and Ben was still Jewish and was again dismissed on the presumption that his presence would cause an international incident. He began to feel like that man without a country.

Chaplains from both Jewish and Christian faiths urged Ben to kick up a fuss, file a complaint, but Ben had no appetite to take on the U.S. Navy, or the U.S. Government. He just wanted to get on ship, any ship.

But it wasn't any ship he lucked into. It was the aircraft carrier U.S.S. Saratoga, CVA-60, the largest ship in the Navy; perhaps the world. Ben was thrilled. He sailed the oceans with 5,000 men and more than 100 aircraft, mostly jet fighters. Not all of it was glory. Pilots landed half-cocked and came in only to drown in flames along with their aircraft. The seamen who worked the flight decks to direct the aircraft incoming and outgoing were equally in peril. In maneuvering the jets their airdales were prone to slip off deck and such men also died in quantities. All were kept frozen in reefers, the ship's huge refrigerators.

As a journalist Ben published the ship's newspaper, put out guidebooks for the sailors and pamphlets for the visitors. His job was closely related to PR. The ship made frequent port calls and when visitors came on board Ben was there to welcome them and explain the inner workings of this magnificent vessel. He liked to say that the ship was a floating city containing everything from barbers to pilots and everything in between.

Ben's other job, his real job, the job he loved, was his battle station function as an enemy airplane spotter.

This was action! Not combat, but action of sorts to be standing out there on the deck with binoculars against the breeze tugging at your denims and nothing but blue ocean and blue sky between you and God Almighty. His past life, his earthbound existence was like a time that never happened. Not once did he think of Louise or Greenwich Village or Cincinnati or Ohio State or Paris or the Roundup or the checkpoints through Gestapo roadblocks or the Catholic orphanage or the nun up in the Pyrenees who wept that there is no God. No, here there was a God, only God.

Maybe once or twice he thought of Louise, the way she had glittered that day and said, Always remember me like this. Always associate happiness with me. Yes, once or twice he did think of Louise and Greenwich Village, but no more than that - he was a spotter after all, the ship depended on him, the Navy depended on him, America depended on him.

The heavens and the deep belonged to him and he rejoiced to be a part of something majestic. There was nothing like it, certainly nothing like it on land. On land only a Biblical shepherd could understand a seaman's wonderful loneliness before the power of nature and timelessness.

At sea the waves carried off time and place and whatever a man was before he could never be again.

The sea got into your blood and even your heart began to beat with the rhythm of the tides.

Out there on the deck as a spotter Ben felt a stirring sense of achievement. He was assigned to the gun deck that contained a contingent of Marines and this only made him feel more valiant and glorious.

In late May they set for the waters off North Vietnam. The mission was mostly secret but as a journalist Ben was privy to some information. The conflict between the South and the North was escalating and the South's guerrillas, parachutists and frogmen kept failing to penetrate communist shore installations. All that despite American advice, assistance and support.

Raids by the South's torpedo boats also failed to damage the North's installations.

By early June the aircraft carrier entered the Gulf of Tonkin - the combat zone. Orders came down to lend moral support for the South's saboteurs without engaging or provoking enemy fire.

The ship was to be on routine patrol, nothing more. From his post on the gun deck, Ben was astonished to find himself in the middle of a war! TV, radio and the newspapers back in the States had it all wrong. Torpedo boat explosives lit up the skies. Artillery shelling boomed across the waters. An armada of PTs could be sighted over the horizon by light and by darkness. Planes went crashing into the deep.

This was war all right and Ben was right in the middle of it, though not quite. The monster ship with its 100 silver planes remained far off the coast and it was there only as a chilling reminder to the North of American firepower.

Show the colors. We're here Ho Chi Minh.

Ben ached for combat. He did not know what the problem was exactly between the South and the North. They both looked the same, except that the North Vietnamese were called gooks. But they were the same people and what the hell the United States was doing here was not for Ben to question or answer. That part of it was for the politicians from Johnson through Rusk through McNamara through McGeorge Bundy.

The gooks were the enemy and that was about the extent of it for Ben and the rest of the 5,000 sailors.

The gooks were from Hanoi and Hanoi wanted Saigon and Russia and China wanted it all, the whole world.

So maybe that's why America was here with aircraft carriers and destroyers on sea and guns and advisors on land. They were here to stem the tide of communism. Made sense. Made sense to Ben - though he did have some qualms. This was a spat between neighbors and perhaps left to their own devices they'd somehow sort it all out between themselves.

Back home, according to the letters, voices were being raised against America's involvement, however slight.

Slight?

That was a laugh among the seamen and the pilots.

From Ben's perspective on the gun deck only hours or days separated his ship from combat. The combat zone was not for cruising. They were still out of range of artillery emplacements but getting closer.

Ben wanted it even closer. Not for the glory but as a test of his manhood.

The test came when nine enemy torpedo boats opened with flames coming squarely at him. He stood his ground. Ben stood his ground and reported the alarm until the entire ship was mobilized and at battle stations.

Ben stood his ground even as enemy artillery shells aimed directly at him and his ship zoomed across the sky. The ship wasn't hit. On orders from the captain the Saratoga took evasive action and cruised away 60 miles from the coast.

But Ben had been hit. The fragment of an artillery shell blew into his right shoulder and left him dazed and bleeding on the gun deck. Medics rushed to his aid and brought him to sick bay, where he was barely conscious and suffering from shock. He remained in sick bay until he was lucid again but the wound, not terribly serious, would require hospitalization, and thus he was shipped to the Philadelphia Naval Hospital from where he was up and out in two and a half weeks.

Two weeks after that he got his medical discharge and soon after three ribbons for valor.

It all happened so abruptly. In the Navy, out the Navy, in the war, out the war.

But what a difference it made! The difference was staggering.

He left for Cincinnati to begin life as an American who had paid his dues.

Even more important, he left for Cincinnati as an American, period!

That was all he had asked of the Navy, and the Navy had given it to him.

Chapter 27

Ben was hired as a general assignment reporter for the *Cincinnati Times*. Managing Editor Gabe Hollendorff welcomed Ben as a refreshing addition since Ben was the only Vietnam veteran on the staff and was therefore in a position to provide a special point of view to what was happening across the nation. Ben was startled to hear himself referred to as a veteran. Hollendorff cautioned Ben against expecting gratitude as a war hero. In only a matter of months everything had changed, as you'll soon find out for yourself, Hollendorff warned - adding that he expected Ben to be subjective and opinionated. His columns would appear on the Op-Ed page.

Ben said he was game. Don't be too game, said Hollendorff. You may be sorry you left Vietnam.

Ben traveled the hot spots and found a nation in turmoil during what was being called the Freedom Summer of 1964. Race riots everywhere and unrest sweeping the campuses of America. The Free Speech Movement, once confined to his very own tidy Greenwich Village, was now rippling across the land, but without the relatively benign face of Bleecker Street. If Lenny was a voice, this now, a year later, was a roar.

Young men and women of college age were beginning to demand freedom to choose their own curriculum, the freedom to frolic in the nude, the freedom to express them-

selves in the vocabulary of their choice, the freedom to protest America's increasing involvement in Vietnam.

On August 7, President Johnson signed the Gulf of
Tonkin Resolution which gave him the power to widen the
war in Vietnam (a war that would take the lives of 45,865
American boys over a period of nine years). Earlier that
month, on August 4, the U.S.S. Maddox was peacefully cross-
ing through international waters when it came under
bombardment from three North Vietnamese PT boats. Such
"unprovoked aggression" inflamed Congress which fell in
line behind the president and set the stage for a prolonged
Vietnam War.

Only later would it be suggested that the Maddox and
the U.S.S. Turner Joy had been sent into North Vietnamese
waters to *incite* aggression from the communists and had in
fact never come under attack. The whole thing had been a
set-up by Johnson and company to rally Congress and the
nation.

Ben had been there, of course, in the very same waters,
and only months before, and he could accept arguments for
or against the events that led to the Resolution, but, for the
movement his heart was on the side of the government's
version. In any case he was a veteran, yes he was a veteran,
and his only thought was to support the boys. He'd been
there and he knew, he knew things these kids would never
know. So he was put off by the vehemence of these campus
protestors who were accusing the government of contriving
a war.

But if Vietnam was a pretext for the Establishment,
these kids - as Ben now came to think of them, though he
was part of their generation in age if not in spirit - these
kids did not need much of an excuse to go nuts.

Things were changing too fast for Ben whose soul was
still back at sea. Women had begun to say fuck. They wore

mini-skirts that covered up practically nothing. They took The Pill. At some campus rallies and sit-ins they went topless.

A generation of rebels and revolutionaries had come of age while Ben's back was turned.

University presidents, accustomed to the submissive Ozzie and Harriet generation of the 50s and the very early Kennedy 60s, gazed out one morning to find themselves confronted by an army of radicals calling for their heads.

Ben Jaffa was baffled. Though he understood why the cities were under siege, he could not get a handle on the campus unrest. The cities were in turmoil because blacks and liberal whites were demanding racial equality. But the campuses - what did these pampered sons and daughters have to complain about?

Ben's editors at the *Times* were delighted with his dispatches "from the front," as the *Times* renamed his Op-Ed column. They were pleased with his contrary point of view, his insights as a veteran and even more important, the use of his impulses as a refugee, an immigrant. He saw it all and described it all as an outsider who had accidentally stepped into a family brawl and finds himself bewildered.

Mostly, he was bewildered by the ingratitude of the young and the privileged.

Ben still thought the ruckus would blow over before too much damage was done.

This was America, after all, a nation with a short attention span, the land of fads. Do the three minutes for the tube and then off for commercial. So, Ben reasoned, all this raging was just another fad likely to go the way of Davy Crockett.

On assignment he hit such flashpoints as Cleveland, Detroit, Chicago, Philadelphia, St. Augustine and of course Berkeley and rather than subsiding over the weeks, the discontent kept gathering speed within the whirlwind of FSM, the Free Speech Movement, which was suspected of being communist.

Ben was at Berkeley when this man Mario Savio of New York laid down the gauntlet. Savio likened the university to a Nazi concentration camp whose purpose, at the behest of the Board of Regents, was to turn Berkeley into a work camp of technicians for the pleasure of the Establishment and its war machine.

That moment in Berkeley triggered sympathetic rioting throughout the nation (and from then on America's campuses were plunged in chaos throughout the 60s). Savio and the rest of them were in their late teens and early 20s but to Ben Jaffa this was a tantrum of the terrible twos.

Equally distressing to Ben was the racial animosity swirling from big city to big city. Black militants were preparing to put America to the torch. Burn Baby Burn. As if that weren't enough, so-called pacifists began burning their draft cards and heading for jail or Canada rather than serve in Vietnam. Another shock to Ben's system of belief that this was a nation of John Waynes. John Wayne himself became a figure of derision. Love of country was trashed and respect for the flag was consigned to the dunghill of quaintness. The flag itself was being torched in ceremonies resembling the bonfire of the vanities.

During scuffles between hard-hats and anti-war militants on the streets of New York, Newark, Boston, Detroit, Baltimore, Philadelphia, Chicago, San Francisco, Los Angeles, Ben found himself siding with the hard-hats, though their taunts, jeers and intimidations too often recalled the Brown Shirts of a more terrible time, a more terrible place.

When all that came visiting back home in Cincinnati, that's when Ben grew alarmed, and furious.

Ben had found an apartment in the hilltop Mount Adams section of town. The place came with a terrific panoramic view of the city that had been named after Cincinnatus, the Roman general famed for his abandonment of war for the serenity of farming. (Rome was Cincinnati's sister city also because both contained seven hills.) In other words, from the outset Cincinnati was all about peace, civility and tranquility.

Cincinnati was Midwest, heartland, grassroots - quintessential America. So orderly, well-mannered and well-behaved was this town that even in the dead of night no pedestrian would cross its spotless streets until the light turned green.

So this was not the place Ben expected to find strife and upheaval.

Mount Adams, though, was a replica of Greenwich Village, the Greenwich Village of 1963 when Ben first moved in. Up and down the hills there were coffeehouses and hootenannies and the smell of espresso and the sounds of Peter, Paul and Mary. Artists, writers and folk singers predominated the scene, and it was all quite peaceful, and then it turned ugly.

Not on Mount Adams, but at the University of Cincinnati, from where the drumbeat of revolution could be heard.

For Ben, the good and the bad all harkened back to Greenwich Village of the year before; Bleecker Street in particular.

The restlessness for change, the call for justice and freedom of expression, the lament against oppression and war, the fad of hipness - he had seen it all first on Bleecker Street.

That's where it all began about a year ago, but then and there it had been so guileless.

Now from coast to coast it was all so hate-filled.

The rest of the nation had copied Greenwich Village - but they got it all wrong.

Pockets of Bohemia were to be found in all the major cities in duplication of the Village scene, but from those centers of weekend hipness there came not the gentle voices for peaceful civil disobedience but rather the harsh wails of bloodcurdling protest.

Down with everything!

America, Ben Jaffa wrote in one of his last columns - was in this throes of a nervous breakdown.

He blamed it all on Lyndon Johnson. The loathing between blacks and whites, between pacifists and hard-hats, between college students and their administrators - such resentments had always been there, but under Kennedy it had been subdued, at least delayed. Kennedy had offered the promise of a new nation, a new frontier. People believed him.

No one believed Johnson. Kennedy had been a visionary, Johnson was a politician, a wheeler-dealer. Kennedy had brought out the best in people; Johnson brought out the worst.

Ben put that in his Op-Ed columns as well but it was not what got him fired.

Those pacifists were burning their draft cards, and the American flag, on the steps of U.C.'s Administration building in protest of everything but most specifically the war in Vietnam. They chanted, "Hell no, we won't go!"

Okay, thought Ben, don't go - who the fuck wants you anyway - so don't go, *but don't burn the flag*!

One pacifist in particular seemed to glory in stomping what remained of the red, white and blue. Ben approached this self-proclaimed pacifist and asked him what he was doing.

"Feels good," said the pacifist.

Ben socked him first in the belly and flattened him with a shot to the jaw.

He finished up by asking, "How does that feel?"

The punk got up, staggering, and took a swing at Ben.

"Pacifist, my eye," said Ben first to the assembled and then to the police who drove him off not to arrest him but to keep him from being mobbed and torn to shreds by the rest of the pacifists.

Hollendorff hated to fire Ben, but the publisher of the *Cincinnati Times* had had enough of Ben's anti-Johnson diatribes.

This publisher was no supporter of Vietnam but he favored Johnson for pushing through the Civil Rights Act of 1964, the legislative high point of the Freedom Summer. Ben was asked to tone it down on Johnson. Ben said no, so Ben had to go.

Anyway, there was still plenty of summer left and Bleecker Street was calling.

Chapter 28

Louise Carmen was back and in full bloom, now, in fact, something of a star. Throughout the year her group, the Highlight Singers, had appeared on many of the networks' variety shows and she had sparkled. She had that clean wholesome all-American look about her, and it was a winner.

Ed Sullivan had been the big break. As a counterweight to rock & roll, which he himself had energized by introducing the nation to Elvis and the Beatles, Sullivan began opening spots for more virtuous entertainment. The All-American Highlight Singers fit the bill.

Louise was thrilled to find Greenwich Village alive again. A year had passed but things were almost the same. The Bitter End was in its place as were the Café Au Go Go, the Café Muse, the Café Feenjon, the Village Gate, the Village Vanguard, the Hip Bagel, the Lion's Head, the Crazy Horse Saloon, the Purple Onion, McSorley's, the Blue Note, the Back Fence, the Dugout, the Pink Pussycat, the Duplex, the Bon Soir, and the restaurants like Patrissy's Asti and El Chico were still humming.

Even the Bleecker Street Cinema was still showing Truffaut.

So it was good and good to be back.

The temper of the place was a bit changed and not completely to Louise's liking. There was still the same languidness by day and the same frenzy by night, still the same rush of creativity as expressed in humor, song and poetry, but absent the exuberance and blithesomeness of before. Conviviality and camaraderie was almost on par, but there was no mistaking a new wave of urgency in the wake of the nation's discontent - and Louise had been out there to witness a good part of that discontent.

Louise had also changed. A year will do that and what a year this had been!

But Louise was not about to complain. Her nightmare had not come true. The Village was still here, still open for business, the business of fun and frolic. What she wanted most of all was to do the summer of 1963 all over again. That's why she had persuaded the manger of the Highlights to decline bigger bucks uptown in order to do the Village *one more once.* Took some talking, but he caved in, as did the rest of the girls in the group.

So Louise was back performing at the Village Gate, kicking it up there on stage to the delight of one packed house after another. Up there in the spotlight she was as zestful as ever and always had them clamoring for more of that tut-tut touch-not-hands-off sexiness.

She had found a sixth floor walkup on Thompson and there, away from the light, she was not always so zestful. In touring the nation with the Highlights she had kept in touch with Richie even as he was being shipped off to Vietnam, and sporadically with Ben even after he had returned from Vietnam. She kept wanting to know where everybody was. Harlan wrote back that he'd failed to make the Chicago Symphony Orchestra but had hooked up with a terrific jazz combo. The streets, however, were not safe. Louise knew that, too.

Louise knew few details about Richie and Ben. Ben had been in and out of the Navy and she did not know how he had gotten in or gotten out. Richie did not say much either in his letters, but at least he kept writing to her. Ben only wrote when he had the chance. That was Ben, Mr. Cool.

In all her letters she pleaded for one thing; that they reunite and do it all over again.

She'd be back and she'd be waiting and it just wouldn't be the same without them, she wrote in letter after letter.

Still by correspondence, she scolded Ben and Richie for deceiving her about the Army, in Richie's case, and the Navy in Ben's case. They had pulled a fast one on her while she'd been away on tour and she'd never forgive them. Never ever. Well maybe if they promised to love her just a little bit she'd reconsider. But you'll never hear the end of it from me, she wrote - but please come back. Even if it's on furlough or whatever they call it in the military.

Ben was not at the Bitter End, she wrote, and Richie was not at the Village Gate, and that was unfair. So unfair.

They'd have to make it up to her, she insisted.

The day of her return to the Village she spotted the marquee at Improv City, stared at it and had to keep staring at it to find Ben Jaffa's name as "co-author." Jimmy Bleeds, that name was in big print. The small print, very small print belonged to Ben.

Well, thought Louise, something is better than nothing and she wondered how Ben would respond when he got back. Would he still care after where he had been? How much do people change after they've been to war? Would Ben be the same? Would Richie be the same? Was she the same or do we all get just one good season in our lives, one season to be young?

A week after her return she took in Lenny Bruce's gig at the Au Go Go and if he was any indication, things were not as okay as she had hoped. Lenny spent most of his act reading his court papers, the *megillah* of indictments and charges that made up his profile.

His asides, mostly against the censorship that was being imposed on him, were solidly on the mark in their withering denunciation of the Authorities but it saddened Louise to find Lenny so obsessed with the Law.

He'd never been that way before. Last year he'd been more accepting of the absurdities that ensnared him. Now he had taken his case to the court of public opinion and these "jurists" at the Au Go Go were not so amused. He was going over the limit even with audiences that came to be titillated and shocked by his outrageousness.

They resented his tasteless comment about Jackie, that she had "ducked fast to protect her ass" when her husband was struck by the bullets. This did not go over well before an audience of Americans still in mourning.

The Café Muse was another sign that things were not terrific. No more long lines for Cliff Harris. No more Cliff Harris - not at the Café Muse and certainly not doing JFK. About Cliff Harris, Louise had heard some evil reports, mainly from Gloria MacKenzie.

Cliff was a beaten man. His comeback sans Kennedy was flopping all over the place. He had finally gotten some off-Bleecker gigs but couldn't keep a job. He'd begun to lash out at the audience for no apparent reason - or perhaps the reason was all too apparent. They were coming to gape at the Kennedy ghost. The people were motivated by nothing more than morbid curiosity. They were lusting for some ghoulish delights.

They still wanted him to do Kennedy and that's what drove him bonkers. I don't do dead people, he cried out.

Others were repelled by the *chutzpah* "John Kennedy" doing Lenny Bruce material, the angry and profane comedy Cliff had been pocketing all along. These zingers - and now he had Johnson trading missiles with Khrushchev - were seen as an abomination and as totally unfitting from the man who had been America's model of Camelot. The people resented this awful resurrection, and thus it was blasphemous for this "Kennedy" to be alive when the real Kennedy was dead, dead and buried in Arlington.

Lenny and Cliff were reminders to Louise that it wasn't the summer of 1963 anymore. All was not perfect.

She herself had not been so pure, either. Yes she had slept with Roger in Wheeling and regretted it terribly. She'd never do it again. She made that exact promise to Richie. Never again. That was her last fling. She was ready to settle down, career or no career, and the man she was ready for was Richie, Richie Bell.

She loved Ben and would always love Ben, but Ben would never be ready. No, she wrote Richie - it's you, it's you that I love and it's you that I want to marry. If that's a proposal, Richie wrote back, I accept. So the plan was set. Richie had a furlough coming and he'd be there on Thompson before the summer was over and they'd get married by his chaplain buddy who'd be coming along. Ben, they agreed, would be best man. Even Ben agreed.

These expectations helped keep her spirits up. She tried not to think of Richie in Vietnam. He had joked - of course he joked, he always joked - about how he was starting to get used to an M-14 on his lap instead of a guitar.

Louise did not think it was all that funny. Pictures were starting to come in about body bags and even though President Johnson kept saying no American boys were going to fight other people's wars, there was this Gulf on Tonkin business and it sure was starting to look like American boys *were* going to fight other people's wars. They were fighting already with boys like Richie and Ben -

and what about Ben? He was out, but was there a chance he'd be going back to the Navy?

These lighthearted letters from Richie and from Ben - while they were still coming - did not fool her. Maybe last year they would have fooled her, but not this year. She'd been out and about and she had grown up. She was not quite mature. She never wanted to *mature*. But she had become a seasoned young lady from her own experiences in combat.

For even here, back home, there was a kind of war going on and she'd been there to see it firsthand.

The America she saw in her travels was split in half, between the young and the old. (Don't trust anyone over 30.) Then it was split again between black and white. Everybody was for something or against something.

The pastoral, small-town, backwoods America of her youth and upbringing still existed but out in the cities and the campuses, where mostly she and her group performed, there was stridency, strife and upheaval.

Even among the young there were fissures; a Pat Boone camp and an Elvis Presley camp. Blue suede shoes versus white bucks. Louise and the rest of the Highlight Singers were decidedly Pat Boone, and for that they paid.

They were jeered and mocked from campus to campus. Their only successes - from which they derived their celebrity - were with the older crowds, to which they were a reminder of things past, or traditional values. They were a bit raunchy, quite sexy - but at least they were not protesting.

At Berkeley and Kent State they were stoned even before they got off the bus. Riding the highways of California, Michigan, Illinois, New York, Pennsylvania, Ohio, the girls were forbidden to so much as leave the bus at rest stops for fear of being raped, abducted or murdered. Black Americans were on a tear. In Detroit their bus was trapped in a riot between blacks and rednecks.

But it was in the South that Louise had her moment of clarity.

The Council of Federated Organizations, the CFO along with SNCC and CORE had organized a thousand volunteers of both races to march on Mississippi for justice and equality. The purpose was to register black voters - nearly a million of them - in keeping with the letter and the spirit of the Civil Rights Act recently passed by Congress and signed by President Johnson.

From reports on television Louise knew all about the proposed march and she knew trouble was expected from white Mississippians, and she also knew that her group had a date in Jackson, June 23.

They got there just in time to be welcomed by chaos in the streets. The CFO marchers were being jeered and beaten. Louise was chilled by the sight of helmeted riot police showing no mercy.

Her own bus - really nothing more than a van, clearly marked *The Highlight Singers* - was mistaken as part of the CFO contingent and was being surrounded by a mob of enraged white Southerners. The driver managed to step on it and find an opening to an alley that scraped the sides of the vehicle as it sprinted for safety like a fleeing rat.

Tensions were especially high - here in Jackson and throughout the South and even across the nation - after reports that three of the marchers were missing. Michael H. Schwerner, white and Jewish, Andrew Goodman, also white and Jewish, and James E. Chaney, a black American from Meridian, Mississippi, had come and gone two days earlier. They were presumed to be murdered.

Then they were not presumed. They *were* murdered after they'd been arrested for speeding in Neshoba County.

Their 1964 Ford station wagon was found only the day before, June 22, 15 miles northeast of Philadelphia, Mississippi. No driver or passengers - but the station wagon had been burned.

This was not the time to be in Mississippi so Louise's bus set out for the highway and even out in the open it was not safe as the Klan Air Force, the KAF, were dropping explosives from the sky along the Delta to target scatterings of CFO marchers. Churches, presumably of black congregants, were aflame from townlet to townlet. Louise watched it all in horror and it would be months before she found out that the three missing volunteers had indeed been brutally murdered.

So this was a chastened and wiser Louise Carmen who now pranced up there on the stage of the Village Gate. Things were different. She was different. In some ways she was the same old Louise Carmen, that mischievous come-hither glint in her eyes, that bouncy step hair swirling as she romped, that ready smile, that quick laugh - all of it was still there, but a beat slower.

Regardless of all that she had seen, and despite the absence of the two main men in her life, Louise would never remain melancholy. She would simply not be as *completely* happy as she had once been. That was all, the only difference between then and now, this summer and last summer. She would not be sad. Never sad. Only less happy, by about a fraction. Just a little bit.

Chapter 29

Ben took a train from Cincinnati to New York. Something about trains thrilled him and chilled him. At about the time of the Roundup in Paris his mom and dad had been on a train, a sleek beautiful train, and he remembered being held by his nanny and waving them goodbye, waving and smiling and loving the train they were on. They weren't smiling back. Then the train started to huff and puff and slowly leave the station and the nanny began to cry.

That was the last he saw of his parents but even now he was not sure if that was how it had ended and his own odyssey began first in the orphanage with his sister and then up the Pyrenees with so many strangers in and out of uniforms.

His memory about the whole experience was very vague and that was how he wanted it, vague. He did not want to know too much about the past and seldom thought of it and spoke of it; to what end? What happened, happened and others had had it much worse.

In America itself, the America of today, children suffered silently from neglectful and abusive parents and that also counted as surviving and even counted as surviving a concentration camp. There need not be barbed wire and watchtowers, only anguish.

He never thought of himself as a survivor but rather as a soldier, always a soldier. He had come of age when Israel became a nation, a nation of soldiers. That was his image of his people and of himself, to the extent that he had even gone over there to serve for the sake of leaving behind a token of himself, that token of blood to bind him with his Biblical fathers.

Now he did not think about that too much anymore, either. Not after serving in the American Navy.

He did think about the French now and then, with mixed emotions, fitting since the French were a people of mixed emotions. They had behaved heroically during the war and they had behaved cowardly during the war, mostly cowardly.

When Hitler's troops came marching in Gentiles had turned their backs on their Jewish neighbors, in many cases betraying them to the Gestapo, and yet it was Christians who had risked their own flesh to save Jewish lives, including Ben's.

So nothing in life was that simple. Most of life was fuzzy and inconclusive. You were born with questions and you died with questions. In between you tried to find some answers but you still died with questions.

Ben's appointment in Greenwich Village was another exercise in vagueness. He knew he had to go back but was not sure why. Thomas Wolfe had already made it a law, so he was not going home again to find things as they were. No, he had unfinished business, namely Jimmy Bleeds. This was not a good campaign and he hated himself for this lust for revenge. But it had to be done. This much had to said for war; it made you forget the rest. Come back and there it is, everything else.

On the good side, the finished side, there was the up-coming wedding of Richie and Louise, and that was a good campaign. Yes it was and Ben felt glad that it had come to this. It was destined all along and it was so right!

Louise, according to her letters, made it seem that Richie's return was a sure thing. Didn't she know that Richie was in the swamps of Vietnam? Didn't she know that you do not just get up and leave, furlough or no furlough?

Probably not, Louise being Louise. Did she think that war was like a 9 to 5 job with weekends off and two weeks vacation? Probably, Louise being Louise. Did she think you could call in sick? Probably.

That's why she was Louise and that's why he loved her and always would. He loved her so much that he was thrilled that she was marrying Richie. Richie loved her even more and Richie, could give her the kind of life that he, Ben, never could. Ben would only ask this, to be named godfather to their children. He had no doubt that they'd consent. That way, in one form or another, they would always be together, bound, if not by blood, then by irreversible friendship.

So that was the real reason for going back, but behind it all was Jimmy Bleeds. Ben wondered if it was in him to take a life. Back in boot camp a bunkmate from Alabama kept staring at him the first day.

He had that grin about him that Ben knew too well. There were no Jews in the small town where he came from, the punk said. He had never seen a Jew before - "so do you mind if I just look you over?" Ben said yes he did mind. Ben said believe it or not Jews do not have tails and Jews did not have horns. Ben said Jews were people just like everybody else. In fact Jesus was a Jew. Yes the Lord Jesus was a Jew and the Lord Jesus did not speak English, the Lord Jesus spoke Hebrew. The Lord Jesus was not born in a small town in Alabama. The Lord Jesus was born in a small town in the land of Israel. Ben said Salk and Sabin were Jews and were it not for Salk and Sabin you, punk, would probably be in a wheelchair paralyzed with fucking polio - which in any case would be just about right.

At this moment Ben knew he had it in him to take a life, and at the same moment he thought of Jimmy Bleeds.

Ben took a cab to Bleecker Street, Bleecker and Sullivan, and he was overcome by nostalgia. He checked out the apartment where they had all stayed the year before and as expected it was rented out.

Different people were living there now; no more Sullivan Street Irregulars. But so much of the Village was still the same, or so it appeared to be on the surface. He found a place on MacDougal, a cold water eighth floor walkup owned by an Italian family that spoke no English. Not much anyway, but the lady landlord knew enough of the language to caution him against drugs and against women. One incident would be enough to evict him. The woman apologized for her deficiency in English. She'd only been in this country 42 years, she explained.

Ben kept to himself for several days. He stayed away from the usual haunts in order to avoid a crash landing from high expectations. He knew it could never be the same, so why go looking for disappointments? In good time he would make his entrance at the Village Gate where he hoped to find Louise as good as new. No chance of running into Richie Bell. Maybe tomorrow, or maybe the next day, if Louise was to be believed from her letters. But Richie was in Vietnam, and Ben knew from being there that it was much worse than people thought, than what people here were being told. Much worse.

Ben had nightmares about Richie returning in a body bag. That was something Louise probably never thought about and maybe that's why Ben was staying away from her for as long as he could. He was afraid that he'd give his fears away. Louise was no dummy. She was sensitive to a look, a pause, a sigh, a faraway glance.

Jimmy Bleeds was another reason not to rush into things. Ben had been nursing that grudge for so long that he needed time to cool down before he did something foolish. He did not want to kill the man. He did not even want his name back on the skit. No, it was too late to make amends. So he just wanted to punish the man, give him a sound beating. He was not worth going to jail for. Or maybe he was. Maybe killing him was the answer. Maybe he ought to kill Jimmy Bleeds as his father had never killed Adolph Hitler. Jimmy Bleeds, after all, was today's Adolph Hitler, Ben's personal Adolph Hitler, the Adolph Hitler every man has at his back.

Ben had to give Jimmy Bleeds this much. The man had been right about plagiarism.

Everybody does it, in speech, in thought, in writing, in music, in art, everybody copies everybody. Except that outright theft was a far cry from unconscious aping. Outright theft was another matter - but no longer so amazing to Ben. His dispatches for the *Cincinnati Times* had been syndicated across the nation and that was fine, even flattering, except that different bylines appeared over his copy. Word for word his copy, with some other reporter's name over the top. Intellectual property was nothing sacred, apparently. So what was?

Jimmy Bleeds knew the score and he had been correct to accuse Ben of being naïve. Well he was not naïve anymore - but it still was not right. No, once you begin to accept small injustices you open yourself to accepting larger injustices and you end up being a man who takes day for night, wrong for right, bitter for sweet, false for true. You become corrupt and Ben was not yet ready to join the crowd.

"Oh, God!' Louise yelled when Ben finally made his appearance at the Village Gate. Actually he had made several such appearances at the Village Gate, but in hiding, keeping to himself in the lobby just to check her out from afar and see whether she was the same old sassy kid, at least up there on the stage, and up there on stage she sure was electric. "Oh, God!" she kept saying while hugging the daylights out of Ben, and then stroking his cheeks and then hugging him some more, finally snuggling up to him, there in her dressing room, and weeping softly, weeping for what was and for what wasn't.

First stop that night was the Hip Bagel and they sat at the same butcher block table they had always sat around, that table against the wall, except that so much was missing. Richie's chair was empty, and so was Sonny's and Lenny's and Cliff's and Joe Franklin's and even Howie wasn't around. Somehow that too was sad. "Shut up, Howie!" That too was no more. Now it was just the two of them and they tried to pretend that they were happy, happy and carefree and full of life as they had been only a year ago.

But it wasn't a year ago. That year was gone and even Louise wasn't so foolish as to believe that it could be done all over again exactly. No, there were bound to be differences and certainly Ben was different.

She wanted to know everything. How handsome he must have looked in his Navy whites! He showed her a snapshot and when she saw that photo of him on the Saratoga first she gasped and then let out a scream of delight. Were there sharks in the waters? Had he seen whales while on deck?

Yes, he said, he had seen it all. Sharks and whales and schools of smaller fish numbering in the thousands.

She did not ask if he had seen gooks. She did not know that that's what they were called. She did not want to know, neither about that nor the fighting. Nothing about the war. All she cared about were the sharks and the whales as though that's what it was all about. That's why American boys were being shipped over there hundreds and thousands at a time, for the sharks and the whales. Nothing about the Vietcong. Nothing about the artillery bombardments and the fear of being blown to smithereens.

He explained about his medical discharge and shrugged off the wound to his right shoulder even though she noticed there was something odd about his right arm. He could not seem to extend it fully and appeared to have trouble gripping knives, spoons and forks. She noticed it but let it go. She wanted to know everything, but really, she didn't. She wanted to know the good parts, not the bad, and Ben was wise enough to understand. Richie was still out there and she did not want to be reminded that there were bad parts to his war.

The following night they took in the Serendipity Singers at the Village Vanguard. In the darkened room Ben put his arm around her and for a tingling moment she wondered if he could still toy with her nipples as he used to, damaged arm and all. But she did not pursue it and neither did Ben. No, it was all very platonic.

The fire was still there between them, but it would have to stay there smoldering and unresolved. Louise was now a betrothed woman and what's more, what's worse, her man was in Vietnam. So there'd be none of that between Ben and Louise.

But she did move out of her Thompson Street apartment to join Ben on MacDougal. The landlord's husband - or whatever he was; talk about an extended family - kept asking "Seester?" whenever Louise walked up with Ben and Ben nodded, yes, "Sister."

In fact that's how they lived together, as brother and sister. The urges were there but that's how it was going to be. Richie was due back any day. Any day now, she was going to be a *wife*. Richie was going to be a husband. "Can you imagine that?" Louise laughed.

"You finally nailed the sonofabitch," Ben said, not asking how definite she was about his return. She seemed too happy about the prospect and in fact it was all she was really happy about. Richie and the thought of Richie as her husband was what kept her bouncing up there on stage and off. Although Ben noticed it, too, that she was a beat slower on stage and off. Her timing was off ever so slightly.

Her moments of delight came between long intervals of silence and her moments of puppy warmth, when she snuggled up against Ben in the apartment or out on the town, were too often sighs of unspoken grief. She was prone to inattention, distraction and bouts of impatience, not as a rule but enough to persuade Ben that her gladness was more measured than spontaneous.

"Let's leave," she said in the middle of Barbra Streisand's performance at the Bon Soir. She loved Barbra, but she simply did not have the patience to sit through a whole show anymore.

After dinner and drinks at the Lion's Head they sat and said nothing for a while. Louise was sulking, and then she brightened. "You came back a hero, Ben. I'm so proud of you." Then she approached the unspoken. "Richie's also coming back a hero, don't you think so? Don't you think so, Ben?"

"Of course," said Ben.

"I only wish I knew what he had to prove. I think I know what you had to prove. I know you better than you think I do, Ben. You had something to prove and you did. I'm so jealous of the girl who's going to marry you some day! I'm warning you, Ben, I'm gonna tear her eyes out. The nerve, the *chutzpah* of the girl, whoever she is!"

"Such *chutzpah* all right."

"But Richie, what did he have to prove? Why did he have to go? What is it with you guys?"

"It's war, Louise."

"But I thought it wasn't a war."

"Well, it is and it isn't. But it's war."

"You're not saying what I think you're saying."

Ben knew it was time to switch tracks. "I'm saying I can't wait to be your best man," he smiled and toasted her.

Louise smiled back, if only half-heartedly.

They sat some more in silence and then tears began to bubble down her red cheeks.

"Louise," Ben said softly, reaching for her hand.

"It's just that - I mean look how we're sitting here and talking but really not talking."

"It's not always smart to talk, Louise. It's not even smart to think and it's sometimes dumb to say what you think. Better not to talk and not to think. You learn that out at sea. You don't think, you don't talk. You just let it happen and what happens happens."

He was preparing her.

"I mean," she said, "we used to have so much to talk about. Now we sit here like *regular people!*"

"Aren't we?"

"No, Ben. We were always so special. All of us. Now we're sitting here like squares. Like tourists." Now she chuckled. "You know what Richie would say. Like Cleveland. But it's true, Ben, we've become Cleveland."

She went on to complain about how so much has changed and even that which hadn't changed was still not the same. Not quite the same.

Greenwich Village was no more their very own secret playground. The rest of the country caught on and that wasn't to the good. Bob Dylan was now nationally famous, as were Peter, Paul and Mary and Joan Baez and Judy Collins and Mort Sahl. Everything was going mainstream and thus losing its punch. Espresso and cider were now being served all over the country upon rickety tables atop sawdust floors. Shelley Berman and Nichols and May were now network and no longer exclusively Greenwich Village. Hardly anything was. Woody Allen was off to Hollywood. Improv comedy was now all over the country after its inauguration right here on Bleecker Street at the Premise Theatre, where Reni Santoni and Louise Lasser and the rest of them used to startle the audience with their dead-on spoofs of a Lenny Bruce-Au Go Go raid by the fuzz.

Ben did not need Louise to remind him of such things past; that what had been good was now being diluted and what was bad was still here. Off on his own he had caught up with Cliff Harris at some dive on Grove Street. The place was half-empty.

There was no sense of mirth. All you heard were cackles for a second-rate clown in a second-rate strip joint. Cliff was mocking LBJ, President Lyndon Baines Johnson - "Maw fellow Merkins, it is with a heavy hurt that while I assure you that no Merkin boys will be sent to fight another   people's war, yes, it is with a heavy hurt that I am sending ten thousand more troops, not boys, but troops, to Vietnam. Thank you maw fellow Merkins and God bless Amerika."

Ben did not show himself to Cliff. He was embarrassed for himself and he was embarrassed for Cliff.

Gloria MacKenzie told Ben that Cliff was hanging on for one reason - Bobby. Bobby Kennedy. Bobby was sure to unseat that swine in the White House, and then, why then it would be Kennedy all over again. Yes, happy days would be here again. (Never, though, at the Café Muse. Never that way again.)

As to Ben's future, Nate Beloff was making a movie in Hollywood, and Gloria assured Ben, Nate would surely keep his promise to find Ben a job writing scripts. I'll think about it, said Ben, but he didn't.

He was still soured by the business of creative writing. Which reminded him...

Chapter 30

Ben had seen his name in small letters on the marquee of Improv City and such tokenism did nothing to calm him, not to deter him from taking action. Early one morning he stood by the door of Improv City with one thing in mind. This much was not going to happen. Talk. Jimmy Bleeds was a good talker and had talked his way out of it last year, but not this year.

No, there would be no talking this time around. None of that nostalgic horseshit that had sedated Ben the year before. The skit was still going strong - the hit of the show. Gloria had told him that if there was one thing that still kept the tourists coming in droves it was that skit. Ben's skit.

Which only served to double Ben's rage. Now that's how he should have and would have gone to Hollywood to join Nate Beloff, as the proprietor of one of the biggest hits in New York, and not a Vietnam vet searching for work, and then only to have another script purloined while he was looking the other way.

So Ben stood there waiting for Jimmy Bleeds and the man finally showed up with his dog. That big black dog. The dog growled and then whimpered and heeled at the sight of Ben. The dog remembered. So did Jimmy Bleeds. Jimmy Bleeds also remembered and offered a smile, a weak smile of fright.

Jimmy Bleeds knew that Ben had come back after serving in Vietnam - and war does something to a boy. Yes he'd heard that Ben was back in town, been back for weeks, and he knew the moment was coming.

Ben floored him right there on the spot. No black belt martial arts stuff. Just a plain old fashioned good old all-American sock to the jaw, and Jimmy Bleeds went down in a heap. Ben helped him up and said these words slowly, slowly so that they should sink in, in their full Biblical resonance: "Put your house in order, Jimmy Bleeds. Put your house in order."

Now that was a death sentence, Biblically speaking, and Jimmy Bleeds knew the weight of such words.

"Message delivered?" said Ben.

"Message delivered," said Jimmy Bleeds, a very frightened Jimmy Bleeds.

Was there anything he could do to change things? he wanted to know.

He was willing to put Ben's name up in much larger lettering.

Ben shook his head no.

Okay. "Then how about we just take my name off and put your name up there - full credit. It's all yours."

"Too late," said Ben, and that was how Ben left it, left Jimmy Bleeds wondering, always wondering and looking over his shoulder. That, to Ben's thinking, was the real punishment, never being safe and never being sure when that knock on the door might come. Now that was terror and Jimmy Bleeds ought to know how it feels. For once, let them know, let them have a taste.

So? Ben asked himself later. What have I achieved? Have I really uprooted all evil from this world, or have I merely gotten one old man to shit in his pants? No, there is no getting rid of them. As soon as one generation of bigots and anti-Semites dies out another generation of them sprouts up and starts all over again.

The weather had much to do with Ben's change of mood. Louise was still holding out for Richie, but Richie still wasn't back, wasn't even writing anymore, and Ben was beginning to wonder what was keeping him here now that it was late September and raining and another summer had come and gone.

Cliff Harris brought it all into focus for Ben. Cliff could be seen teetering along Bleecker Street smashing whiskey bottles and shouting epithets at pedestrians and passing cars.

"Maw fellow Merikins," he kept muttering.

Both Louise and Gloria MacKenzie asked Ben to please talk to Cliff. Somebody had to do something.

Ben got him to the Hip Bagel and there Cliff was almost lucid. "What you're looking at," Cliff said, "is the mirror of America. That's me, and that's what people want to see. I'm a reflection. What they did to Kennedy they did to me and it sickens them. I sicken them. I frighten them. My very features, my *face*, is a reminder to them of a transformation they created. They created me, this monster, as they created Johnson. Lyndon fucking Johnson. They turned me into Johnson and they turned themselves into Johnson, and that's why they hate me. That's why I hate me. I've become an abomination to the people and to myself. You know how people cleansed themselves of sin back in Biblical times? They took this goat, see, and they turned him loose in the wilderness. That goat was supposed to carry off all their sins. That's where we get the term scapegoat. They've turned me loose into the wilderness to avenge their sins."

In that case, said Cliff, "Fuck 'em all. I'm dropping out. I'm going into the mountains to study witchcraft."

Which he did. (By mid October Cliff Harris was gone, dallying somewhere in the mountains of Vermont to join a Satanic cult. Then he moved on to join the flower children, followed by the hippies and then the yuppies as one movement replaced the other. Everyone seemed to be joining movements and cults. He meandered to Haight Ashbury where he got hooked on LSD and then, after Charles Manson, when the flower generation became synonymous with drugs and murder, Cliff Harris retreated and became a Jesus Freak, unaware that he was duplicating his father.)

All right, so he had taken care of Cliff, had talked to him exactly as Louise and Gloria had requested - and only made it worse. Cliff was irreclaimable. Cliff was about as hollow and washed up as a man could get. But Ben had tried, only to find himself reflected in Cliff's mirror.

Ben was almost as hollow as Cliff, and it took Cliff to remind Ben just how aimless and purposeless he'd been since leaving the Navy and returning to Greenwich Village.

Ben even forgot why he'd come back. Then he remembered that he had come back to recapture the glory that had been the summer of 1963. That, and Louise, Louise being the catalyst to make it all happen again.

That's why he came back, but why was he staying? Again, Louise. Ben was her lifeline to Richie and the good times. Ben was her lifeline period. She had moved in with him to keep him near her memories. That was one reason. The other reason, the real reason, was to stop him in case he woke up one morning and decided to pack up and leave.

That would surely devastate her, plunge her into that suicidal despair that kept hovering over her eyes. That's why Ben was staying. He was waiting for something to get resolved, then he'd move on, perhaps to Hollywood after all. That, or something else. Maybe he'd go back to Cincinnati, a wonderful city, a great town, but a town without a beat or rhythm.

Back in their apartment on MacDougal, Louise was a wonderful companion. She cooked, washed the dishes and made the beds, anything to keep Ben happy, to keep Ben staying. She told him about all her experiences on the road and admitted to being frightened about what was in store.

But life goes on, she said. She'd begun to buy clothes for her honeymoon. Ben told her that that was back luck.

"Oh," she said, "you and your Jewish superstitions."

No, Ben said, it's plain bad luck. Like you don't buy clothes for a baby before the baby is born. You don't tempt fate. Louise said she did not know anything about fate. Fate was something writers and philosophers worried about. Fate had nothing to do with her or Richie.

"So stop being a ninny and come with me to Fifth Avenue," she'd say.

Ben refused. He'd have no part of that, no part of tempting fate, not with Richie in Vietnam.

He told her as little as possible about Vietnam - besides the whales and the sharks. She was not willing to listen anyway. When he'd bring up the subject - only to let her know that real people with real guns were shooting at one another and not at the whales and the sharks - she'd turn her head and stare out the window.

But she continued to buy clothes from Saks Fifth Avenue and bring them back and try them on and twirl delightedly in front of the mirror, a full length mirror that hung by the living room door and was cracked down the middle. That was another thing that Ben was superstitious about.

The older a man gets, Ben was thinking, the more superstitious he gets. Some call it finding religion but it is really a gnawing mistrust of all things rational. When the world stops making sense you tend to reach out for the absurd since it is only the absurd that makes sense.

Not that Ben was old. He was very young. But the chronology of years had nothing to do with being young or old. He'd forgotten about the war he'd been born into and the war he'd just left, but it added up.

So he forgot about all the events that had made him old. He forgot about them as much as possible. He even forgot to say *Kaddish* for his parents once a year. The prayer for the dead was something that prompted even agnostics and atheists to rush to the synagogue once a year on Yom Kippur. They double-parked, rushed in and out, but they remembered. Ben forgot.

Sometimes, though, he did wonder why he'd been spared. He above so many others who had perished. Did fate - the same fate Louise mocked - did fate have something in mind for him? Did he owe his parents gratitude and was this gratitude to be paid by some marvelous achievement? If so, his destiny had yet to be revealed to him.

He had fought bravely for Israel and now, finally, for America. Maybe that was the payment. Maybe he had already achieved something marvelous. But there was still more life to live and could this be all? Had he done it already?

Though he was at odds with most of his generation, those privileged "Hell no we won't go, down with everything!" kids throwing a tantrum from campus to campus, he was very much like them in his pursuit of meaningfulness, meaningfulness being a word much in play and therefore trite - but still, there was something to it beyond shouting.

There had to be something else besides business as usual, status quo. That was, or had been, Greenwich Village. That's what lured them here, with Ben at the heels. He had expected to find his destiny here, and came close, but not close enough.

It had been one hell of a ride, a wonderful ride, and he would remember every minute of it, but in the end there'd be nothing more to it than remembrance. Memories. Terrific and wonderful memories.

Greenwich Village, specifically Bleecker Street, and specifically Richie and Louise and Sonny and Lenny and Cliff the way he used to be, had opened his eyes to a world of gentleness.

Yes, gentleness. These were such fragile souls, even Richie who presented himself as invulnerable.

* * *

Ben and Louise were at the Hip Bagel when Richie's parents dropped in. What a surprise! Ben had never met them, but Louise had during a stopover in Hartford. Mr. and Mrs. Bell had at first been put off by the thought of Richie marrying someone besides Sally Caruthers, but one visit was all it took to persuade them that Louise was the one. They were dazzled by her show biz flair, but that wasn't it so much. She was so down-to-earth, so homespun, that they could not resist her - and so lovely, too. She'd be the perfect match for Richie, both of them so full of life.

Mr. and Mrs. Bell. So stereotypically middle-class, or rather upper middle-class, but typical nonetheless of the traditional over-30 husband and wife who had grown up and thrived in an America that adhered to a value system of Duty, God and Country.

Old-fashioned, in other words, and out of sync with the times. Nothing wrong with old-fashioned, to Ben's thinking, and to hell with being in sync with the times. No, nothing wrong with these people at all. These were the people that kept the country humming, and kept it on its pegs. Without them - yes, the silent majority - without their heroism in war and sacrifices in peace America would not be America. Only their allegiance to the flag, to home, family and hard work made it possible for their kids to have the means and the leisure to rise up and revolt.

Mr. and Mrs. Bell. Ben knew why they were here. Louise jumped up to hug them one at a time and Mrs. Bell returned her affections by sobbing softly as Louise abruptly let go and retreated gasping.

"No," she said. "No. Please no. Please don't tell me. Oh God, please. No no no."

Louise ran off and disappeared. Mr. Bell, still standing, explained to Ben that Richie had been killed at an air base in Bienhoa, 20 miles north of Saigon. He had died heroically in a firefight.

Richie was dead. For Louise, Greenwich Village was dead. The carefree, flamboyant, lively, creative, devil-may-care spirit that was Bleecker Street was now coming home in a body bag from Bienhoa.

Chapter 31

Word spread quickly throughout the main streets and byways of Greenwich Village that one of their own had fallen. A son of Greenwich Village had passed away. Richie Bell was eulogized in song and poetry from bistro to bistro. But a week passed before the Village gathered itself in official remembrance at the Café Muse, this so that Louise Carmen could recover from delirium tremens. Gloria permitted Cliff Harris to take the stage at the Café Muse one last time. Cliff was in no condition to veil his bitterness. He finally had a packed house again and his grieving was both singular and general.

Richie's demise, said Cliff, was the symbol of America's decline and sorrow. The assassination of John Kennedy was a line drawn in the sands of American history. On that day last year, November 22, 1963, America lost its soul. America was changed forever. Nothing would ever be the same. Our blessed nation had turned into a cursed nation just as John Kennedy turned into Lyndon Johnson.

Now this generation and all generations to follow were destined to suffer the consequences of the sins of their fathers. The torch had been passed from goodness to evil. The bread of affliction, this now was America's portion.

In conclusion, Cliff could not resist one last jibe. "Maw fellow Merkins," he said.

Ben Jaffa followed with Louise Carmen at his side. Ben read from David's elegy to Jonathan:

"Thy glory, O Israel, is slain upon the high places. How are the mighty fallen. Saul and Jonathan were comely and pleasant in their lives. And in their death they were not divided. They were swifter than eagles. They were stronger than lions. Ye daughters of Israel, weep over Saul, who clothed you in scarlet delicately, who put ornaments of gold upon your apparel.

"How are the mighty fallen in the midst of battle. O Jonathan, slain upon thy high places. I am distressed for thee, my brother Jonathan. Very pleasant hast though been to me. Thy love to me was wonderful. How are the mighty fallen, and the weapons of war perished."

Chapter 32

Cliff Harris left the Village in a swirl of disgrace. His eulogy was met with derision after he used his moment not only to grieve but also to mock President Johnson. Cliff departed in haste - but for another reason.

Jimmy Bleeds was dead and it was not Ben Jaffa who had done the deed. Jimmy Bleeds had been looking over his shoulder all right, for Ben, not for Cliff. Cliff was the man who killed him.

Cliff hurt for Ben. Ben, mostly Ben, had stood up for him when it counted against Ed Sullivan. Ben had saved his career and now, Cliff reasoned, he would return the favor, even though Ben had no need, no desire and even no knowledge of Cliff's favors or intentions.

No, Cliff did it all on his own. Measuring his own fall, Cliff was prepared to martyr himself for Ben, to sacrifice himself for the sake of the righteous. Cliff was, of course, largely incoherent at this point of his life, but he clearly knew that he had lost the tiny foothold each man plants for himself.

He had naively believed that he had never been a comedian, nor even an impressionist, but rather a messenger of lovingkindness. Kennedy had merely been his stage prop to spread the message. With Kennedy gone, lovingkindness vanished; only the Jimmy Bleeds of the world remained.

Cliff chose November 22, 1964 to step in and strangle Jimmy Bleeds to death.

Thereafter Cliff Harris became a hunted man, stalking the wilderness like a true scapegoat. His four-year odyssey through the subterranean cultures of America paralleled Cain's wanderings in pursuit of peace and shelter after his brother Abel's blood cried up to the heavens.

But Cliff found no inner peace and only occasional shelter in the various cults he joined. He tottered from wilderness to wilderness. He attached himself to bizarre religions and experimented with exotic drugs. But there were no cities of refuge for him. He was on the run from the law, from his countrymen, but mostly from himself.

(In 1968, when it all came completely undone for everyone, Cliff, harkening to the voice of Jesus once again, surrendered himself for the murder of Jimmy Bleeds. After serving three years in a federal penitentiary in Pennsylvania he resumed his career, but as a marginal, minor, talent, a man, like a million others, always on the verge of a comeback. Unlike the others, though, Cliff was doomed to eternal failure since the luminous glory he had once reflected lay buried in Arlington.)

* * *

They were at Penn Station caught amid the multitudes, two stunned figures blurred against the backdrop of a thousand welcomes and farewells, a handsome young man, a pretty young woman, together and apart. The echo of arrivals and departures, of trains coming, of trains going, quickened them to shared memories and to the singular destinies that awaited them. For a moment they touched. For a moment they smiled. For a moment they embraced.

"We will keep in touch," said Louise.

"I promise," said Ben.

Their trains were being called, but separately.

"Promise again," said Louise, holding Ben tightly and sobbing.

"I promise," said Ben.

"I love you, Ben," she sniffled.

"I love you, too, Louise."

"Just a little bit?"

"Just a little bit."

She attempted a smile. "I told you. Everybody goes away. We all go away. Didn't I tell you?"

"Yes, you told me."

"So I was right, wasn't I?"

"You were right."

"Why is it people are always right about the bad things, Ben?"

"I don't know. I really don't know."

"Always the bad things."

"Not always, Louise."

"Next year, Ben?"

Ben knew there'd be no next year. Not in Greenwich Village. So did Louise.

But to depart like this, without the illusion, that would be something entirely too brutal.

"Next year, Louise."

"We were good, weren't we?"

"We were the best."

"Remember us like that," she said. "Remember us at our best."

"That's a promise."

"And do you remember what I told you?"

"What?"

"Oh, Ben, you forgot."

"What?"

"That day last year when we were all sitting around at the Café Muse and it was all so wonderful, and then the news came that Kennedy..."

"Oh, to always remember you like that, in happiness."

"Not quite. I asked you to always associate me with happiness. Whenever you're happy, think of me."

"I will."

"Promise?"

"Promise."

"You won't forget."

"I won't forget."

He turned his head for a moment to listen for the final announcement of his train.

When he turned back she was gone.

Amid the crowd he could only make out a trace of her bobbing black hair, a sight that used to delight him.

Yes he would remember. Even now he'd begun to remember and was not sad. In his mind's eye he saw her face and she was right, he was happy. He would always associate her with happiness. Always.

* * *

Author's postscript:

I'm told that Greenwich Village is alive again. Bleecker Street is humming and the Bitter End is back. I'm sure it's true, and for all I know things may even be better than they ever were.

But it will never be the same.

www.ingramcontent.com/pod-product-compliance
Lightning Source LLC
Chambersburg PA
CBHW031122030726
47496CB00002BA/653